WHERE
BUGLES
CALL

Between Two Flags

An American Adventure

9802

WHERE BUGLES CALL

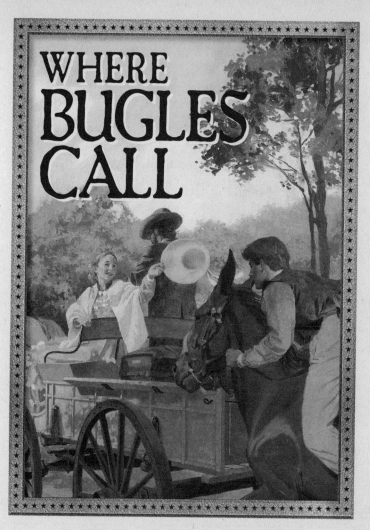

LEE RODDY

BETHANY HOUSE PUBLISHERS
MINNEAPOLIS, MINNESOTA 55438

Where Bugles Call
Copyright © 1998
Lee Roddy

Published by Bethany House Publishers
A Ministry of Bethany Fellowship International
11300 Hampshire Avenue South
Minneapolis, Minnesota 55438
www.bethanyhouse.com

Printed in the United States of America by
Bethany Press International, Minneapolis, Minnesota 55438

Library of Congress Cataloging-in-Publication Data

CIP data applied for

ISBN 0–7642–2026–8   CIP

To my grandniece,

Tanya Kniespeck,

who knew what she wanted
when she was only about eight,
and persevered until she succeeded.

LEE RODDY is the award-winning and bestselling author of many books, television programs, and motion pictures, including *Grizzly Adams*, *Jesus*, and THE D.J. DILLION ADVENTURE SERIES, BHP's AN AMERICAN ADVENTURE, and THE LADD FAMILY SERIES with Focus on the Family. He and his wife make their home in California.

CONTENTS

PROLOGUE

From Gideon Tugwell's journal, October 12, 1933

As I mark the first day after my eighty-fifth birthday, I continue with the story I began yesterday about what it was like to be a child during 1861–65. That's the period now commonly called the War Between the States or the American Civil War.

I refresh my fragile memory by again opening the faded pages of the daily journal I kept during those terribly bloody years. More American servicemen died at that time than in all of our wars since—more than 600,000 on both sides.

The faint words from those brittle pages recall for me the people, places, and events of almost seventy years ago. Families were torn apart, old traditions were trampled, political beliefs were tested, black and white races were thrust into deep conflict, and all of that was recorded in human blood.

But it is not just my penciled words that spark scenes of so long ago; rather, it is a girl's hair ribbon that marks my page. That once-pink ribbon, now faded with age, instantly recalls stirring incidents and memories of people; especially three people.

In memory I see the boy Gideon (that was me back then); Emily, the Yankee girl trapped in the Confederacy while visiting there; and the slave boy Nat.

We were each from totally different cultures, yet the war

★ ★

wove us together as if we were mere threads in the great tapestry of that tragic conflict.

I have already told you about how the war started for us and how our own little worlds were already being changed forever because of the first great land campaign fought in Virginia. Yankees call it Bull Run, but we Southerners refer to it as the Battle of First Manassas.

What happened next is now flooding back to my mind, stimulated by words I wrote so long ago—plus a piece of pale ribbon. The war was the background, but the story is about those three people who were caught up in the next events.

Here is how it happened and how I wrote it day by day—where bugles called.

A DESPERATE NEED

It was bad enough to repair a split-rail fence in the muggy weather of late July, but it was worse for young Gideon Tugwell when he had to work with his hard-to-please father.

"No, Gideon!" he roared, throwing down his hammer and striding the few feet to look down on his twelve-year-old son. "I've told you a thousand times not to do it that way! Can't you ever do anything right?"

The old familiar anger and resentment shot through the boy. He tried so hard, but there was no pleasing his stern, hard-working parent. Gideon didn't reply for fear of being lashed with even more irate words when his father grabbed the long rail and shoved it into place.

"There! See! It's easy!"

It's easy because you love farming, Gideon thought, *but I hate this hardscrabble place! As soon as I'm old enough, I'm going to move away and—*

Suddenly Gideon heard the sound of a galloping horse coming toward them on the public road. He lifted his black slouch hat from straw-colored hair to wipe perspiration from his freckled forehead. "Papa, he's turning in here and riding awful fast in this heat."

"That's Tom Welch from the village," his father said, dropping the hammer and shading his brown eyes to squint against the July sun. "Bad news, I'm thinking."

★ ★

"Isham?" Gideon asked fearfully. "You think—?"

"Don't say it!" Mr. Tugwell broke in sharply, starting to run to meet the rider.

Gideon followed his father, fearful of the message the rider carried. Isham Tugwell, Gideon's older half brother, was a soldier in the Confederate army. There had been no word of him since the Battle of Manassas the week before near Bull Run Creek in northern Virginia.

"Mr. Tugwell! Gideon!" the young rider shouted as he drew close and reined in his lathered horse. "You heard the news?"

"What news, Tom?" Mr. Tugwell asked, stepping to the side of the sweating animal to look up at the rider.

"Isham's name has just been posted on the village bulletin board. He's wounded!"

"Wounded?" father and son exclaimed together as Gideon's heart twisted in sudden fear.

"At Manassas Junction," the rider cried excitedly. "When we whipped the Yankees and sent them skedaddling back toward Washington!"

Mr. Tugwell's gray-streaked beard quivered on his chin. "How bad is he?"

"I don't know. There's just his name listed under 'wounded.' Nothing else. My pa said you'd want to know, so he sent me to tell you right away!"

"I'm obliged," Mr. Tugwell said softly. "Reckon we ought to tell my missus. Would you like a drink of cold water from the well and rest a spell?"

"Thanks, no. Pa said to hurry back. I'm powerful sorry about Isham." The rider whirled his mount about and started back down the dirt road at a slow trot.

Gideon and his father looked at each other, their faces showing the pain and fear that had suddenly erupted inside them. Then they began running toward their small house where it was well hidden in the trees near the river and partly protected by Black Water Swamp.

★ ★

When the rider's message was repeated inside the small kitchen, a hush fell over Gideon's mother, younger brother, Ben, and sisters, Kate and Lilly.

"Is he going to die?" Lilly whispered with the innocence of a four-year-old.

"Of course not!" her older sister exclaimed.

"We'll pray that he's going to be all right," their mother said reassuringly. She lifted Lilly from the wooden floor and snuggled her to her chest.

From where he sat beside Gideon on the homemade bench, Ben asked, "Papa, what're you going to do?"

Gideon thought his stoop-shouldered father looked suddenly old and tired where he sat by the fireplace. His face was ashen where the beard didn't cover it.

"I'll see Isham when I go back to Centreville to dig up the gold we got for our early wheat."

"What's gold?" Lilly asked from her mother's lap.

"It's money," Ben replied. "Thirteen twenty-dollar gold pieces worth two hundred and sixty dollars. That's more than some folks around here make in a whole year. Even privates in the army like Isham only earn eleven dollars a month."

"Ben!" his father said sharply. "That's enough." He shot a meaningful glance at his youngest daughter before saying, "Remember that walls have ears and lips that speak out of turn."

"Who's going to hear?" Ben replied, turning back to Lilly. "Don't you remember?" he continued. "Papa had to hide it when the wagon tipped over and Gideon got hurt while our soldiers were beating the Yankees at Bull Run Creek."

"I heard," Lilly replied.

Ben continued. "They ran all the way back through Centreville on their way to Washington, and Papa and Gideon rode home on Yankee horses when their owners got killed. Papa buried—"

"Ben, you talk too much!" his father yelled.

★ ★

Gideon had been yelled at so much that he felt sorry for his little brother, even if he did speak out of turn.

Their mother asked her husband, "When will you go?"

The anguish of knowing his oldest son was wounded showed in the father's weathered face. "I had planned to leave this weekend, but now I'd better start tomorrow."

"I'll go with you," Gideon volunteered, anxious for any excuse to get away from the hated farm chores.

"No," Mr. Tugwell said with a shake of his head. "I'll make better time alone."

Gideon protested, "But, Papa—"

"No!" his father snapped. "You stay here!"

From thirteen years of experience, Gideon knew that it was useless to argue with his father, but that didn't stop the anger from bubbling up inside the boy.

Mr. Tugwell rose from his chair. "Now," he said with finality, "there's no use standing around here talking anymore. We've all got chores to do. Let's get back to them. Ben, I'll help you fix that chicken coop. Gideon, you get back to that fence and try to do it right."

Gideon nodded but waited until the door had closed behind father and little boy before turning to his mother. "I hate this place, Mama! Papa is always riding me because I can't do anything to suit him! I want to get away, even if only for a few days!"

"Now, dear, you mustn't talk—"

Ben interrupted her by bursting through the door, his eyes wide with fright. "Mama! Come quick! Something happened to Papa!"

★ ★ ★ ★ ★

One glance at his father's pale face greatly alarmed Gideon. His father clutched his chest where he had collapsed on the back porch steps. His two hunting hounds whined anxiously as he grimaced with pain.

★ ★

"It's nothing," he said. "I just got a little short of breath all of a sudden." He forced a reassuring smile. "I guess I got a little too upset over Isham."

"Do you have chest pain?" his wife asked anxiously.

"No. It's a kind of heaviness, like a pressure here." He touched the left side of his chest. "It's just a little uncomfortable, that's all."

"Should I go for Dr. Janssen?" Gideon asked.

"No!" His father's word was sharp. "You know we can't afford a doctor! I'll be all right in a minute."

Gideon met his mother's eyes as she said, "Just the same, I think we should let ol' Doc—"

Her husband broke in firmly. "I said no!" He stood a little wobbly. "Now, stop fretting over . . . oh!" He clutched the center of his chest by the breastbone and sat down hard on the steps while perspiration popped out on his forehead.

His wife bent over him but spoke to Gideon without looking at him. "Ride for the doctor! Fast!"

★　★　★　★　★

Hours later, old Dr. Janssen stepped out of the tiny bedroom where Gideon's parents usually slept. The entire family rose silently to hear his diagnosis.

He closed the door and said matter-of-factly, "It's his heart."

"How bad is it?" Mrs. Tugwell asked anxiously.

"Too soon to tell, Martha. I've done all I can for him for now. He keeps saying he's got to get to Manassas to see Isham, but I told him that's foolish talk."

Gideon glanced at his mother and knew she was suddenly torn between two desperate needs: to keep her husband alive and yet recover the gold. Originally, it had been intended to help the family through the winter. Now it would be needed for the family's survival and urgent medical care for her husband.

Dr. Janssen, always in charge, said, "Martha, you come into

the kitchen and I'll give you instructions. You children better go outside and play or do your chores."

There was a howl of protest, but their mother motioned for them to obey. "Not you, Gideon," she said as he reluctantly started outside. "You stay with me."

Mrs. Tugwell led the way into the kitchen and motioned for the doctor to take her husband's chair. She and Gideon sat apprehensively on the edges of the homemade bench by the plain wooden table.

Mrs. Tugwell asked in a low tone, "Tell me the truth, Doc. Is he going to be all right?"

"I can't say for certain, Martha. But if he wants to live, he's got to stay in bed awhile. He's certainly not in any condition to go anywhere."

The doctor rummaged through his black bag and brought out some vials of pills before continuing. "He's always been about the most stubborn patient I've ever had. Moments ago, while I was treating him, he kept saying he had another reason to get to Manassas and he wouldn't stay in bed. I told him that I don't care what's on his mind, he's not going to leave this house for a while. You've got to keep him quiet, Martha. Do you understand that?"

"Yes, of course."

"Good!" Dr. Janssen handed her the pills and directed her in how to use them while Gideon turned and looked out the window at his siblings. Their frightened faces were pressed against the glass. If their father died, how would they all survive?

After the doctor's old mare pulled the black buggy out of the yard, the younger children rushed back into the house. They fired anxious questions, looking for reassurance. Their mother comforted them, then sent them outside again before turning to Gideon.

"I'm sure I don't have to tell you what a terrible situation

★ ★

16

we're in," she began, her voice low so that her husband couldn't overhear.

"I know," Gideon assured her. "I already figured it out. We're going to need that gold, and fast. I'm the only logical one to go get it, but Papa buried the coins while I was unconscious, so how can I find them?"

"He'll have to draw you a map." Mrs. Tugwell stood up and adjusted her apron. Her voice was still low but strong. "It's too risky for you to go alone, yet I haven't been able to think of anyone who could go with you. Do you have any ideas?"

"I've already thought about all that, too, Mama. I'll have to do it alone."

She whirled from the stove, where she had started to feed more wood into the firebox. "You're only twelve! I can't let you do that!"

"I'll be thirteen in October," he reminded her. "Some boys joined the army who are even younger. Besides, we don't have time to look for someone. If Papa can draw the map, I'll leave tomorrow and be back in a few days."

The two hounds suddenly began baying down the lane.

"Can't be the doctor coming back," Gideon decided, going to the window and lifting the curtains. "Oh no! It's Barley Cobb! He must think it's suppertime and he's come for another free meal!"

"Now, Gideon. That's not a very Christian-like thing to say. After all, he's a widower with no children. . . ."

"He's a slave catcher who's too lazy to cook for himself; that's what he really is," Gideon said without thinking. "I'll tell him Papa's sick." The boy hurried out the door, but his real reason was born of fear that one of his sisters might mention the gold. Gideon didn't trust Cobb at all.

The dogs and three children swirled around the unshaven and dirty man who made his living running down fugitive slaves and returning them to their master for rewards. Gideon had seen slavery all his life, although his father never owned

★ ★

any. Gideon had also heard how Cobb and his dogs mistreated captured fugitives. That sickened the boy because he wouldn't even let his hounds tear up a raccoon or other animal that way.

At just under six feet tall, Cobb was his usual disreputable-looking self. His battered slouch hat covered uncombed, shoulder-length brown hair that matched his untrimmed, to-bacco-stained beard. Below his tattered, homespun shirt a piece of rope belt held up his baggy pants. His scuffed, knee-length military boots kicked up dust in the lane as he walked toward Gideon.

"Evening, Mr. Cobb," Gideon said, hurrying forward in the gathering dusk. "I guess you already heard that Papa is sick."

"So your little brother and sisters were telling me," Cobb said, spitting tobacco into the dust. "I'm powerful sorry to hear that. Now, if there's anything I kin do—"

"Thanks," Gideon broke in. "But he needs rest and quiet, so I can't even invite you in to visit with him."

"Just the same, I'd be mighty proud to come in and see if there's something the missus needs a man to do."

"Thanks anyway, but Ben and I can handle everything."

"Well, if you're sure." Cobb shifted the wad of chewing to-bacco to his other cheek and looked longingly toward the house. "Not much smoke from the chimney, huh?"

"We've been so worried about Papa that Mama hasn't started supper." Gideon almost smiled in spite of himself when he saw the look of disappointment on the man's whiskery face. He had an uncanny knack of showing up just at mealtime, when there was no polite thing to do but invite him to take a place at the table.

"Besides," Gideon continued, "we're all late doing our chores. I have to milk the cow, and Ben's got to fix the chicken coop before dark to keep the foxes out."

The slave catcher licked his lips and sighed softly in dis-appointment. "I'd stay and help you boys, but I just stopped by on my way over to Briarstone. One of the Lodge family's slaves

★ ★

done run off, so I got to get my dogs and go bring him back."

Gideon hoped the runaway wasn't the slave named Nat who was owned by William Lodge of Briarstone Plantation. Although only fifteen, William ran the big tobacco plantation while his father, Silas, was away serving with the Confederate cavalry.

Unknown to any white person except Gideon, Nat's previous owner, now dead, had secretly educated him. There was great risk in that because it was against Virginia law for a slave to be literate. Nat had helped Gideon improve his own reading and writing skills when he couldn't attend school.

"Which slave?" Gideon asked as casually as possible.

"Don't know yet." Cobb took another longing look at the Tugwells' home. "Well, I got to be going." He turned away, then stopped. "You want I should say howdy for you to William's sister and her purty Yankee cousin?"

Even though Gideon had saved Briarstone, it didn't take long for William's attitude to sour again. He still forbade Gideon to speak to either his sister, Julie, or their cousin Emily, who had come from Illinois to live with them.

"No, thanks," Gideon said. He took his two little sisters by their hands and started back toward the house.

Little Lilly called over her shoulder, "My Papa is going to dig up some gold he hid when—"

"Lilly!" Gideon cried, instantly clamping down hard on the little girl's arm. She cried out in surprise, but it was too late. Cobb spun around, his eyes wide.

Lilly kicked Gideon in the shins. "Why did you do that?" she demanded indignantly.

"Never mind!" Gideon almost had to drag her away. He glanced back and saw that Cobb had not moved. Even in the gathering dusk, Gideon was sure he saw a greedy look in the man's eyes.

"Lilly," he said softly, lifting her onto the porch, "I sure hope you don't get us in a lot of trouble over that remark!"

Ben and Kate ran into the house first, shouting to their mother about what Lilly had said. Mrs. Tugwell shushed the children, then motioned for Gideon to come with her into the lean-to where the girls usually slept.

Looking at Gideon with deep concern, his mother asked, "Do you think Mr. Cobb heard her?"

"No doubt, Mama. You should have seen his eyes. I've got to be going after that gold first thing tomorrow."

"Do you suppose he'll try to follow you and take it when you dig it up?"

"I don't trust him, but he said he had to chase a runaway slave at Briarstone. Maybe he won't have time."

Mrs. Tugwell sighed. "I've heard him brag that he could follow a shadow across the Potomac."

"We don't have a choice, Mama! We've got to have that money as soon as I can get it. You know that!"

"Yes, I know." She gently laid her work-hardened hand against his cheek. "But I feel terrible even thinking about you being out there all alone with all that responsibility, even if he doesn't follow you."

"I'll be careful, Mama. I can do it."

Slowly, she nodded. "Then we have no time to lose. I'll see if your father is feeling up to drawing that map. Ben and I can handle the chores until you get back with the gold and a report on Isham's wound. You can start at first light."

Gideon walked outside, lit the lantern, and carried it and the milk pail toward the barn. He had never been away from home alone before. He was scared but didn't want his mother to know because she had enough to worry about.

At the barn door he paused and looked off into the distance. Faint glows in the windows at Briarstone showed the kerosene lamps had been lit. Gideon shook his head. *I sure hope it wasn't Nat who ran away.*

Besides the beating that Cobb would give him, and the way his hounds would chew Nat up, William was sure to give his

★ ★

body slave a terrible whipping. Then, as he had before with other runaways, William would probably sell Nat so far south down the Mississippi River that he could never again hope to escape to freedom.

With an effort Gideon forced those thoughts aside and tried to concentrate on his own urgent mission.

THE THREAT

A shriek outside the big house at Briarstone awakened Emily Lodge. She sat up suddenly in her second-story bed-chamber as the cry of pain echoed from the barn and other outbuildings, then died away. She lay back down, her violet eyes looking up at the white canopy over the high four-poster bed.

A second cry jerked her upright, making her long blond hair bounce across her face. She brushed it aside and slid off the high bed. She put on carpet slippers and a pale green dressing gown before dashing out the door and down the hall to her cousin's adjoining room.

"Julie!" Emily exclaimed, bursting in without knocking. "Did you hear that?"

The dark-haired girl in her bed waved a hand in dismissal. "It's just my brother with one of the servants. He ran away yesterday, but the slave catcher and his dogs caught him last night. So go back to sleep."

Emily stopped in disbelief beside the bed, which was a duplicate of her own. "How can you say that, Julie? Listen to that poor slave screaming! I can't stand it!"

"Don't you dare interfere!" Julie warned. "William is feeling his power while Papa's away, so even Mama and I won't dare oppose him."

Emily clamped both hands over her ears as the shrieking

★ ★

continued. "I've got to stop him!"

"No!" Julie sat bolt upright. "You can't risk making William angry! If he turns you out, you've got nobody else to take you—"

Her sentence was left unfinished as Emily rushed out the door and down the long hallway.

Emily raced down the curving staircase and out the huge paneled front door of the three-story brick manor house. It was square and solidly built, with graceful white Corinthian pillars supporting the two-story front entrance and a balcony on the second level. Urged on by the cries from the slave quarters well in back of the big house, she dashed past the new Confederate flag flying from one pillar and streaked down the graveled path between neat English box hedges.

The field hands were usually in the tobacco rows at dawn, but now they stood in a silent circle, forced to watch punishment for one of their members who had tried to run away. The slaves respectfully parted for her, and she quickly reached the site of the whipping post.

It stood upright in the hard ground. A young black man's hands were stretched high above his head, where they were secured by two leather cuffs. His bare back was streaked with fresh stripes, which bled from the wide cowhide whip yielded by Lewis Toombs, the white overseer. William Lodge, standing as master in place of his father, who was away fighting the Yankees, was a few feet away, watching the punishment.

"William!" Emily shouted, running toward him. "Please stop him!"

Her cousin spun toward her, his face red with sudden anger. "This doesn't concern you! Get back inside!"

"What did that poor man do to receive such—?"

"He ran away," William cut her off, grabbing her roughly by the forearm and yanking it hard. "I'm making an example of him! Now, get back inside! I'll deal with you later!"

William gave her a shove that sent her reeling toward the

★ ★

stone-faced slaves gathered around. None dared offer to catch her, but they parted so that she stumbled and fell, tearing her dressing gown.

As she regained her feet, she heard William say to the overseer, "Get on with it."

Emily ran back the way she had come, followed by the whistling lash of the whip and the anguished screams.

★　★　★　★　★

When it was over and William dismissed the assembled black men and women so they could return to their duties, the old gray-haired slave named George fell into step beside Nat, William's young body servant.

At about age fifteen, Nat was a handsome, light-skinned mulatto who shared some of his unknown white father's facial features, so he could almost pass as a Caucasian. His dark, kinky hair distinctly showed his African heritage, so young William insisted he never wear a hat when off the plantation with him.

Nat and George, like all the blacks who had been forced to witness the whipping, walked away in silence. George had been given the honorary title of "Uncle." He was the carriage driver at Briarstone and dressed each morning in splendid green livery with gold buttons on his swallow-tailed coat and matching pants. He was ready at a moment's notice to harness the matched bay team to the magnificent coach with the Briarstone crest on the door.

When man and boy rounded the livery stable out of sight of the others, Nat broke the silence. "What will happen to him now?"

"He'll likely be sold down the river."

Nat swallowed hard. Every Virginia slave dreaded being sold down the Mississippi. That would put the person so far south that there was no hope of ever again trying to escape north to freedom.

★　★

George said softly, "I warned Cyrene not to run away last night, but he wouldn't listen. He didn't get far. A slave catcher named Cobb with his friend Oakley Odell and their dogs caught him."

Nat had been at Briarstone only a short time, so he was still amazed that the old coachman spoke the slave dialect in front of the white folks, but he could speak correct English when he chose. Nat was also impressed with George's talent for discerning what others missed.

"Why shouldn't he try escaping to freedom?" the youth asked, keeping his voice low, although no one was near enough to hear. Nat had made one unsuccessful try for freedom but had returned without being detected.

George rubbed his frizzled gray hair and chuckled softly. "Three good reasons. First, young Master William was home, so he could call the slave catcher right away. Second, did you see how his dogs chewed up Cyrene?"

"I took a quick look." The wounds to legs, arms, and neck were different from the long stripes left by the whip, but Nat knew every one was equally painful. "What's the third reason?"

"He should have gone into the swamp. That would slow the hounds down. Of course, there are other dangers there, like poisonous snakes and wild animals, not to mention the mosquitoes and getting lost."

Nat studied the old man through dark, suspicious eyes. "Then why should he have even thought of going into the swamp?"

"Because of the ghost."

Nat laughed. "There are no such things! That's something the white folks make up to scare us so we won't run away into that place."

"It's true that most of us colored people are afraid of ghosts, real or not. But some white folks are, too."

"I didn't know that."

"A lot of the pattyrollers are. Barley Cobb, for instance."

★ ★

26

Nat stopped in surprise. "Cobb, the slave catcher?"

George also stopped to look the younger slave in the eye. "Yes, both him and his helper, Odell. When I'm driving the white masters in the coach, sometimes they talk as if I wasn't there."

"Are you saying that you've heard them say Cobb believes in swamp ghosts?"

"Heard it many a time." George started walking again. "But nobody of our people on this plantation knows that except you and me."

"Why're you telling me?"

George shrugged. "Just making conversation is all."

Nat didn't believe that but nodded as if agreeing.

George added thoughtfully, "Of course, a person can't hide forever in the swamp. He'd be a fool to go in there without some idea of how he was going to find his way north to freedom."

"That would be foolish," Nat admitted, sensing that the old slave was sharing ideas that could cost them both dearly if it was ever known to the white owners.

"It's only a rumor, of course," George continued in a very quiet tone, "but I've heard that sometimes a runaway comes out of the swamp just in time to have some abolitionist white folks start him on a secret way to a free state."

"Some rumor," Nat replied, his voice almost cracking with sudden hope.

"Underground Railroad, it's called, but it's no railroad at all. Abolitionists around here who don't believe in slavery act as 'conductors,' helping runaways from one place to another until they reach freedom. It would go mighty hard on them if the other white folks found out what they were doing. Mighty hard."

Now Nat was sure that George was trying to tell him something yet be very discreet. "I'm sure it would."

"Most white folks talk around us colored people like we are

★ ★

nothing more than animals or pieces of wood. But not aboli-tionists. That's why I heard their railroad is going to start north in a few days."

Nat stopped dead still. "You believe that?"

"Can't tell you where I heard it, but I believe it."

Hope surged through the slave boy like a living flame. "Starting from near the swamp, I suppose?"

"More than likely." George resumed walking. When Nat fell into step with him, the old man mused, " 'Course, I didn't hear exactly where, but probably some white folks will say some-thing in front of me so I could find out exactly in a few days. Not that you're interested, but like I said, I'm just an old man talking to pass the time."

"I've got to be getting into the house before William does," Nat said.

As Nat started to turn away, the old man called out softly, "When I drove the young master next door to Darlington Plan-tation yesterday, I saw a boy who looks enough like you to be your brother. He was about twelve or so, I'd guess."

Rufus! Nat thought, stopping suddenly to stare at George. Nat's mother, sister, and three younger brothers had recently been sold at auction after their first master died. All had gone to different owners, but Nat planned to escape his own bonds, then return to the South to find and rescue them. It was a huge undertaking, but George's news gave Nat hope. It was the first and only clue Nat had to where any of his family might be.

Trying to keep his voice from showing any real interest, Nat asked George, "Field hand or house slave?"

"Field, I think. At least, I saw him with the older field hands. Well, I'll talk to you later."

Nat hurried toward the big house, his steps suddenly light with hope. For the first time since his family had been sold at auction earlier this year, Nat saw not only an opportunity to escape to freedom, but perhaps to take one of his siblings with him.

★ ★

But how could he make sure the neighbor boy was his own brother? A slave caught off of the plantation without a pass was subject to apprehension and beating by the white ruffian patrollers called "pattyrollers." The captured runaway would also be whipped by his owner and maybe even sold.

Nat made two quick decisions: He would have to see this neighbor boy. If he was Rufus, they might escape into the swamp together. If it wasn't his brother, Nat was going to run away on his own. But first he had to carefully think through what Uncle George had said. Was he telling the truth? Or was he setting a trap?

★   ★   ★   ★   ★

William Lodge was still furious when he stomped into the dining room after supervising punishment for the captured fugitive slave. Emily rose from the breakfast table, where she sat with Julie and her aunt Anna.

"What got into you, Emily?" he demanded, striding to stand directly in front of her. "Father and I overlooked it when you interfered at the auction where we bought Nat, but what you did in front of the servants this morning is unforgivable! You disgraced me!"

"I didn't intend to—"

"Don't interrupt!" William stormed on. "It's bad enough that some of our neighbors whisper behind my back that you're a Yankee spy. But to act like a Northern abolitionist in front of the servants is unforgivable."

"Spy?" Julie repeated. "Who says Emily is—?"

Her brother swung toward her. "Stay out of this, Julie!"

She lowered her head and gazed toward her plate.

Aunt Anna, as usual, said nothing. Emily had never known her aunt to contradict her strong-willed son any more than she would have opposed her husband before he saddled his thoroughbred horse and rode off to war.

"I told you once before," William continued, again facing

Emily, "you don't understand our ways. I can accept that because we Southerners certainly don't understand how you Yankees can try to destroy our system of economics, which is dependent upon free black labor."

Emily met his gaze without blinking or lowering her eyes. She wasn't defiant but simply stood her ground.

He ranted on, "It's impossible to understand how that tyrant Lincoln can try to force his way of life on us when all we want is to be left alone! But I will not have a traitor in this house!"

"Traitor?" Emily exclaimed in surprise. "I've never done or said anything to make you say that, William!"

"That's what it must look like to my friends, and now even to the servants! I'm going to tell you for the last time, Emily, don't you ever again say or do anything to shame me!"

"I did not mean to do anything like that. I just tried to stop you from beating that poor man."

"Man?" William stormed, his eyes crackling with indignation. "Slaves are not people! They are property. The United States Supreme Court said so in the case of that runaway slave Dred Scott a few years back!"

Emily knew about the infamous Dred Scott decision from the highest court. It had ruled that the fugitive was property and was returned to his owner.

"I'm sorry I offended you, William," Emily said quietly but with firmness. "I appreciate your taking me in after my family died—"

"That's another thing!" he broke in again. "I know we're the only living relatives you have, and we took you in out of Christian charity. But if you want to be turned out of Briarstone—"

"No, William!" his sister cried, jumping up from the table. "Don't say it!"

"I'll say it." His voice dropped, but the anger was still there, hard and cold. "Emily, if you interfere one more time with these servants, you are no longer welcome under this roof! Is that clear?"

★ ★ ★ ★ ★

Gideon was delayed two hours in getting away from the farm. His father was reluctant to let the boy go alone on such a long, risky mission. Finally, convinced that there was no other way to recover the desperately needed gold, he carefully went over the map he had drawn so that Gideon would be able to find the gold double eagles where they had been buried under a white pine tree at Centreville near Manassas Junction.

Gideon didn't remember the last time his father had hugged him. He reached up from his bed, so Gideon bent down toward him. He was surprised when his father just shook hands with him. Then he fell back, suddenly breathing hard and clutching his chest.

"He's having another attack!" Gideon cried. But his father insisted it was nothing and he would soon be all right. Still, Gideon and his mother stayed at his side until the pain passed and he slept peacefully.

Finally, with the sun climbing into the morning sky, Gideon placed his meager supplies of food and water in the saddlebags slung over the back of Hercules, the family's big new mule. Gideon also carried a frying pan, a pot, a knife, a fork, a spoon, and a blanket. With his father's precious map inside his shirt, Gideon accepted his siblings' hugs and his mother's kiss.

"I'll pray for you every day and expect you back in about four days," she promised as he mounted. "I'll pray that you find your brother and that you bring the money back safely as fast as you can. Maybe you'll run across that nice black man who helped your father save your life when the wagon overturned."

"Thanks, Mama." Gideon clucked to Hercules and started down the dusty lane with the two family hounds following. They turned back when Gideon reached the public dirt road.

★ ★

He kicked his booted heels into the mule's sides and set a fast pace.

"Hurry up, Hercules," he whispered. "We've got a mighty important job to do and a tight deadline."

Gideon's blue eyes probed in all directions for any sign of Barley Cobb. Satisfied that he wasn't being followed, Gideon sighed with relief and glanced off to the right. In the distance Briarstone manor house rose like a brick island above the bright green rows of tobacco. It was much too far away to see anything more than movement where the field hands worked among the broad-leafed plants.

Gideon thought briefly about Emily with the long golden curls before turning for a final look back. A lone horseman emerged from the woods, heading toward Gideon, but was too far away to be recognized.

Is that Barley Cobb? Gideon wondered. He turned the mule off the road into an open field, heading toward a dense stand of trees in the river bottom. There he could hide and wait to make sure he wasn't being followed.

TROUBLE CASTS
A LONG SHADOW

Emily hurried toward the river, where she could be alone and think. She couldn't stay in the house after the harsh encounter with her cousin William.

She felt a sense of peace among the cottonwoods, alders, and willows and headed toward the quiet murmur of the stream, ignoring briars that snagged her hoopskirt.

I've got to get away from here! But how can I get passes through the picket lines into the North?

If she could get home to Illinois, her best friend would take her in. Jessie Barlow and her mother had always treated Emily like family. They would have an extra room now that Jessie's older brother, Brice Barlow, had joined the Union army.

Emily didn't sense danger until a horse nickered. She glanced toward the sound and gasped. Four saddled horses tied to a low tree branch had the distinctive U.S.A. brand on their hips. They obviously belonged to a troop of Federal cavalry, but none of them were in sight.

Although she was a staunch Unionist, Emily knew that she faced jeopardy if they saw her. She glanced around, her mouth suddenly dry. She caught the sound of splashing in the nearby river, although she couldn't see the men.

Pulling her skirt as tightly about her as possible, she started easing back the way she had come.

She sucked in her breath and stopped dead still as a young,

shirtless man wearing dark blue pants with yellow piping down the legs stepped out from behind a tree. He held a cavalry carbine in his right hand.

"Well, now!" he exclaimed. "What have we here?"

"I'm from Illinois and support President Lincoln," she said quickly, speaking around a lump that had suddenly formed in her throat.

"Oh, is that a fact?" There was mockery in his tone. "That's why you're here in the heart of Rebel country all by yourself? Wait, don't tell me! I know! You're a spy!"

"I told you the truth! My family all died, so I came to live with my only relatives—"

She broke off in great alarm as two other Federal cavalrymen walked up from the river, where they obviously had been washing up.

The one with the weapon leaned it against a tree trunk and put on his loose-fitting shirt before turning to the new arrivals. "Boys, we caught ourselves a young Rebel spy. Don't military regulations say spies have to be hung?"

Emily knew they were teasing her, but that didn't ease her concern. She berated herself for having gone off alone. It had been frightening enough shortly after the North was severely defeated at Manassas that a troop of Federal cavalry, cut off from retreat, had come to Briarstone and threatened to burn it.

All three of the cavalrymen now facing Emily had no marks of rank on their sleeves, indicating they were privates. There was no officer to command them.

One of those who had come up late said softly, "You're going to be a mighty pretty young lady."

She didn't reply, but the sentry who had first seen her commented, "You're sure right about that, Henry. Did you ever see such long blond hair?"

"Who're you talking to?" another male voice asked from closer to the river.

He stepped into view and stopped, staring at her. "Emily? Is that you?"

For a moment she didn't recognize him.

He hurried toward her, buttoning his shirt. "It's me, Brice! Brice Barlow! Jessie's brother from home!"

"Brice!" Emily gave a glad cry and rushed toward him. "I thought you were in the infantry!"

"Transferred," he replied as the other troopers stepped aside to let her pass. "Now I'm a horse soldier."

"I'm so glad to see you!" she exclaimed, smiling with relief. "These men don't believe I'm a loyal Unionist! They're talking of hanging me!"

Brice laughed the way Emily remembered when she and his sister had joked with him in Illinois before the war began. "They're just teasing," he assured her. "Boys, I can hardly believe it, but this is Emily Lodge, my little sister's best friend from home."

The other troopers' attitudes immediately changed toward Emily. They politely acknowledged the introduction, which she returned with a joyful smile before she faced Brice again. "Did you get my letter?"

"No. Did you get mine?"

"Yes. You asked me to pray for you, so I wrote back and said I would! Oh, Brice! I never was so glad to see anyone in my life!"

"Same here." He smiled broadly, looking down on her with obvious pleasure. "You're growing up!"

"I'll soon be thirteen."

His smiled faded and his tone sobered. "If I had received your letter, I would carry it with me through this war. Lots of men have keepsakes to help them remember someone back home. Say, I don't suppose you have a miniature or a picture of yourself that I could have?"

"Don't rob the cradle, Brice," the trooper named Henry said dryly. "She's just a little girl."

★ ★

Brice grinned good-naturedly at the other man. "You're just jealous. Besides, by the time this war is over and we all get home, I might just marry her!"

The men hooted and laughed, but Emily felt herself turn crimson. She glanced away in embarrassment.

The first soldier who had spoken to Emily glanced around anxiously. "Brice, you can stay here and talk to your friend all you want, but the rest of us had better skedaddle before some Rebel sees us and starts shooting."

"You're right," Brice agreed. "All right, mount up."

As the men turned to obey, Emily noticed for the first time that he wore a stripe on his sleeve.

"We're deep in Rebel country," he told her, his voice soft, "and we're separated from our command. So if you could point the way toward Bull Run Creek, we'll be on our way."

"Of course." Emily quickly supplied directions.

"Thanks," he said, lingering a moment longer. "I hope we meet again under more pleasant circumstances."

"I hope so, too," she murmured, her heart aching at the thought of what could happen to him.

He waved and rapidly rode off with his companions.

Emily stood watching until the drumming of their horses' hooves faded away and the silence of the river bottom returned.

She snapped out of her reverie at the muted sound of more hoofbeats moving down from the road, coming toward her from behind. She whirled to see a lone mule and rider. She tensed, ready to run toward Briarstone, then recognized Gideon Tugwell and relaxed.

★　★　★　★　★

At the edge of the woods near the river, Gideon twisted in the saddle for a final look back. Whoever was following was far back, but still coming. Gideon urged Hercules into the shade of the trees.

If it was Barley Cobb, the boy had to somehow escape from

him in the river bottom's undergrowth.

When Gideon reached the deepest shade under the trees, he tied Hercules behind some brush, ran several yards away, and took cover behind a downed log.

He waited, his eyes probing the shadows, his ears alert for any sound. Only the whisper of the river, the rustle of leaves, and the morning calls of songbirds broke the silence.

After a few minutes something moved through the underbrush. Gideon watched, expecting Barley Cobb to appear under the trees. But it wasn't a horseman coming.

Surprised, Gideon stood up. "Emily!"

She whirled to face him, lifting her long skirt above her ankles as though to run away. "Oh!" she said in relief. "It *is* you! I was pretty sure I saw you coming, but you still frightened me."

He leaped over the log to approach her. "I didn't mean to. What're you doing down here all alone?"

"I needed to think." She glanced around, then added quickly, "I just saw some Federal cavalrymen over there."

"Then you'd better get out of here fast!"

"They won't bother me, but they might harm you."

"Why? Do Yankees kill boys my age?"

"Well, no, but they're lost and nervous, and they might shoot first if they see you."

He frowned. "How do you know they're lost?"

She hesitated before answering. "They asked directions toward the north. Now, please leave before they see you."

The unwelcome stubborn streak in Gideon made him shake his head. "Not until you tell me why you came down here by yourself."

With a deep sigh she explained, "I tried to stop William from whipping one of the slaves. I should know better by now. He grabbed me and threw me into the others who were watch—" Her voice broke. She regained control, adding, "I can't stand it anymore. I've got to get home to Illinois."

Anger at William made Gideon's blood run hot, but he didn't want Emily to leave. He could only say, "I won't tell anyone."

Over her shoulder she whispered, "I'm sorry. I didn't want anyone to see me so upset. I wouldn't even let Julie come with me."

She turned to face him, her eyes glistening with new tears. "I just had to be alone, so I came here."

Gideon wanted to comfort her but didn't know how. He lowered his gaze and awkwardly kicked at a fallen leaf. "What are you going to do?" he asked.

"I think I've made a decision." She brushed the tear streaks from her cheeks and took a deep breath. "I just don't fit in down here, Gideon. I'm thinking about going back to Illinois to live with Jessie Barlow. She and her family have always treated me like one of them."

"If you decide to go, when will you leave?"

"I'm not sure. I would need passes. Through my uncle, Aunt Anna knows Jefferson Davis and most of the generals, including Robert E. Lee. So she could help me get through the Confederate pickets guarding the roads to Richmond, but I don't know how I could get passes from there to cross Union lines. Still, I've pretty well decided that I'm going to try."

Gideon frowned, not liking that at all. But he asked quietly, "When's the soonest you might go?"

"Four or five days. Why?"

Gideon hesitated. She had enough concerns without knowing that his father was very sick. Gideon had promised him not to say anything to anyone about the gold. "We just learned that my older half brother was wounded at the Battle of Manassas. I'm going to visit him."

"Oh, I'm sorry! How badly is he hurt?"

"We don't know."

"How long will you be gone?"

"Maybe four days if I'm not delayed." He remembered

Barley Cobb and glanced fearfully back through the trees, but there was no sign of him. Maybe he hadn't been the horseman Gideon had thought was following him.

"Well," Emily said, "I've got to be getting back. If somebody saw us talking together and told William—"

"I know," Gideon interrupted. He had been warned by William to never speak to Emily. He considered Gideon and his family to be "poor white trash," and he and his father had repeatedly tried to buy the Tugwells' farm to get them out of the area. Gideon wanted to tell Emily that he hoped she would still be here when he returned but couldn't find the words.

They stood in awkward silence until Emily finally said, "I should have told you that one of those soldiers I talked to was Brice Barlow. . . ."

Gideon cringed at the name. "You mean the older brother to your best friend in Illinois?" Gideon's voice rose as he remembered some time ago when he had posted Emily's letter addressed to that name.

"Yes. He—"

"Shh! Listen!" He whirled around to look back the way he had come. Through the trees he saw a shadowy figure of a man on horseback cautiously riding toward them, his gaze sweeping the underbrush.

"Somebody's following me!" Gideon whispered. "I've got to go so he doesn't see us talking. I don't want word to get back to William and cause you any trouble!"

Gideon ran as silently as possible to the mule, untied him, and leaped into the saddle. Without even a glance in her direction, he rode off through the underbrush.

★　★　★　★　★

William sent Nat to have George harness the team in preparation for a drive. Nat hurried past the neat English box hedges to the slave quarters in back of the manor house. He passed several small vegetable gardens that slaves tended

★　★

before dawn or after dusk when their plantation work was done.

Uncle George and an attractive teenage slave girl wearing a simple shift carried a heavy wooden bucket between them. They set it down on the path when Nat ran up and delivered his message.

"Thanks, Nat," the old coachman said. "I've got to go before young Master William gets angry. Nat, would you mind carrying this bucket into the cabin for Sarah?"

"Glad to," he replied and lifted the water without the girl's help.

She nodded her thanks but didn't speak. She led the way into one of the many sixteen-by-eighteen-foot slave cabins standing in long rows. Her right ankle was a mixture of old scars and fresh abrasions from the heavy iron shackle she was forced to wear for trying to run away a year earlier.

"How long have you been at Briarstone?" Nat asked, trying to draw the girl into a conversation.

She shrugged and opened the cabin door but remained silent. She had not even spoken to him when Uncle George introduced her to Nat some weeks before, but that didn't discourage him.

As William's body slave, it was risky for Nat to delay returning on an errand. But Nat was attracted to Sarah. She was about fourteen with delicate features and skin much the color of Nat's. She was well on her way to becoming a beautiful woman.

It was dark inside the windowless structure except for low flames in the fireplace at the back wall. Nat placed the water on a rickety old table with two homemade and unmatched chairs beside them. Four corn-husk pallets lay on the wooden floor where she shared living space with other girls her age. The room smelled of woodsmoke from the rude fireplace.

"Thanks," Sarah said and held the door open for him to leave.

"I'd like to talk to you," he said, stalling.

She met his brown eyes with her own but did not reply.

Nat tried again. "Uncle George told me that you and an older man named Pete ran away but got caught."

Nat paused, remembering the terrible sight of a network of whipping scars on Pete's back. "I'm sorry," Nat added when Sarah remained silent. "I shouldn't have asked about it."

He started through the door but stopped when she began to speak. "We should have gone to the swamp and waited for the Underground Railroad. It was a mistake to just head north, following the star."

Nat nodded, knowing she meant the North Star, which many slaves used as a guide toward freedom few ever reached. "I've heard there is such a thing," he said, lowering his voice so no one else could overhear.

"Slave quarters are full of rumors," she continued, also dropping her voice. "I heard that there is a white abolitionist in the village who is planning to help some of our folks to leave for freedom in a few days, if anyone wants to risk running away."

Excited hope suddenly gripped Nat. "Is that so?"

"I told you, it's a rumor."

"But someone around here must know more."

"I said too much already." She glanced toward the pail of water, then back at him. "Thanks again."

Hurrying back to the big house, Nat's mind filled with questions. On an impulse he turned off toward the carriage house, where George lived above the various vehicles.

George was the only slave allowed off the plantation, and then only as driver for William or Silas Lodge. While waiting with other drivers for their masters to finish a meeting, George and his fellow reinsmen had a chance to share what they had overheard from inside the carriages.

"Uncle George," Nat said to the old man finishing the harnessing of the matched bay team, "I heard that there are some abolitionists—"

"Shh!" George cut him off, nervously glancing around. He warned in a voice so low that Nat barely caught the words, "I heard some masters say they suspect Mr. and Mrs. Yates in Church Falls are."

Hope surged in Nat like a hot drink on a cold day.

"I also heard that in about four or five days, one or two of our people who want to risk running could be picked up by the Underground Railroad and start north to freedom. But I'm too old to run," George added.

"I was just curious," Nat hurriedly declared.

George nodded. "And I was just passing the time."

Nat waved to the old reinsman and ran back toward the big house as hard questions battered his thoughts.

Even if the Yateses are abolitionists, how can I make contact with them since no slave is allowed to leave the plantation? How can I be sure if the boy at Darlington really is Rufus? And if it is, could I talk to him alone and see if he's willing to risk escaping with me?

Nat entered the big house, his heart beating faster at the dangers and more questions that bombarded him.

When and where in the swamp will the Underground Railroad start? How can I get away from here without getting caught?

He shuddered at the thought of what terrible things mean white men and their vicious dogs would do to him.

★ ★

DEADLINES FOR THREE

As the sun crept higher in the summer sky, Gideon frequently glanced back, but there was no sign of anyone following him. *Maybe it's just my imagination because I sort of expected Barley Cobb to follow and try to take the gold from me when I dig it up.*

Gideon was so relieved that he was tempted to forget about Cobb and think only of his own pressing needs. He had to see how badly Isham was wounded, find the buried gold, and bring it back to help pay his father's doctor bills and save his life. He had to do it all quickly and before Emily left for Illinois. But getting careless if he was being followed could ruin all of Gideon's plans.

In an hour the dirt road curved around a stand of trees. As soon as Gideon was sure he was out of sight of anyone following, he turned Hercules into the woods and dismounted. He welcomed an opportunity to stretch his muscles and watch his back trail without being seen.

The birds had ceased their morning songs, so the woods were quiet except for a woodpecker drilling on an old, dead tree.

"Whatcha doing, huh?"

The voice behind Gideon made him spin around, his hands automatically coming up to a defensive position while his heart leaped into his throat.

★ ★

A dirty, ragged boy about the age of Gideon's little brother stepped back, his arms raised to ward off a blow. "Don't hit me! I ain't done you no harm!"

Gideon's heart eased down from his throat. "You scared the daylights out of me!"

"Didn't mean to." The boy was short under a man's hat that came down to rest on big ears that were only partly covered by long, stringy hair that was as brown as dirt. "Why you lookin' back the way you come?"

Relieved that it wasn't Cobb who had sneaked up behind him, Gideon managed a friendly smile. "Just making sure nobody was following me, that's all."

The boy tipped his head back so he could see from under the oversized hat. Gray eyes locked into Gideon's blue ones. "You run away from home like me?"

"No. I'm going to see my brother who got wounded at Manassas."

"You are?" The boy's voice brightened. "I'm goin' there muhself to jine up with the army."

Gideon suppressed a smile. "How old are you?"

"Twelve." When Gideon's eyebrows raised in obvious doubt, the boy added quickly, "Well, I'm really goin' on 'leven, but I got to get in the army so's I kin eat regular. My ornery old uncle, he's done whacked on me with a rope too many times whilst he was drinkin'." The boy lifted his torn shirt and turned so Gideon could see the ugly black-and-blue welts on his back. "I run off."

Sympathy made Gideon ask, "What about your folks?"

"Both dead an' buried two years ago. Don't nobody care about me; not even God."

That shocked Gideon. "Don't say that!"

The boy shrugged. "I ain't seen no sign He does. Say, you sure got a mighty big mule tied up over yonder."

"His name's Hercules because he's so strong."

"I heard about Samson in the Bible who was a strong man,

but I never heerd of no Hercules."

"He was a Greek character from long ago."

"Well, I reckon your Hercules could carry us double real easy."

Gideon started to shake his head, but the boy rushed on. "Seeing as how we're both headed for the same place, and we both don't weigh no more than one full-growed man, seems to me we could both stand some company on the way."

Gideon was sorry for the boy, but riding double would slow the mule and possibly lead to disaster.

"I'd like to," he explained, "but—"

"Oh, please!" the boy interrupted, his face puckering as though he was about to cry. "Don't make me walk all the way." He pointed to his shoes. They were far too big for him, and the soles were coming loose. "I won't be no bother! I'll feed and care for the mule, and I got my own food! Fact is, I'll share it with you."

Gideon took another look down the road. There was no sign of Cobb. "Oh, all right. But we have to ride hard!"

★　★　★　★　★

Emily and Julie stood by the fireplace in the Briarstone library with its walnut-paneled walls and shelves of books protected behind glass doors.

"Really?" Julie exclaimed, her eyes wide with excitement. "He said that when the war is over and you both get home, he would marry you?"

Emily regretted having told that part about her encounter with Brice Barlow, but it was too late now. "Actually, he said he might, but he was joking."

"What if he wasn't? Oh, Emily! That's so romantic!"

Emily turned to look at the low flames in the fireplace. "I'm too young for romance. I want to have lots of beaus before I get serious about anyone."

"Not me! When the first boy asks me, I'm going to accept.

★　★

I can hardly wait to get away from this house!"

"That's a wrong reason to marry. I know William's not easy to get along with, but at least he's your brother and he would look out for you."

"Sometimes I wonder. You've seen how he treats me. Not like a sister, but more like another servant."

"In his father's absence, he's feeling the power of being the young master of Briarstone. But at least you're part of a real family. I don't have anybody."

"You have me."

"Yes. I'm glad, but being with my only living relatives isn't the same as a family. I still have a very lost and lonely feeling inside because in a very short time, disease claimed my father, mother, brothers, and my home. Everything that was familiar."

Sighing softly, Emily added, "I guess that's why I have this urge to go back to Illinois, even if my family is dead. It's home, and I do have my friend Jessie there, so I could stay with her. But I want to leave here on good terms, if possible, so I'm trying to get permission from your mother and brother."

"You're making me sad," Julie said with a catch in her voice. "Let's not talk about that anymore." Her tone again took on excitement. "How did Gideon react when you told him what Brice had said?"

"I started to mention it, but Gideon suddenly said somebody was following him, and he rode off real fast."

"Why would somebody follow him?"

Emily shook her blond curls. "I don't know."

"Don't trouble yourself about Gideon. William and Papa say he's nothing but a poor white farm boy who won't ever amount to anything."

"I don't agree. There's something about him that's . . . well, different."

"You don't know him well enough to know that."

Emily didn't like the edge in her cousin's voice. "I know he plans to become an author and write stories."

★ ★

"William will have a fit if he catches you talking with Gideon."

Emily didn't want to think about that, so she said, "I'm sorry to bring it up again, but I've got to go home to Illinois."

Julie reached out and took her cousin's hand. "You know I don't want you to leave here. Please don't go!"

"I don't want to leave you, but I just don't belong here. As your father said before he joined the cavalry, I don't understand the Southern way of life. I never will. But you grew up in it, so you've accepted the fact that some slaves are whipped cruelly or worked to death without drawing one free breath in their lives."

"They're servants," Julie said coolly. "Servants."

"Servants work for wages and can come and go. Slaves cannot."

"But they're fed and clothed and never have a worry in their lives!"

"Don't they? Remember when we were with your father and brother when they bought Nat as William's body slave? Do you remember that poor black mother who pleaded with the bidders to buy her children, but they wouldn't? You know that the mother and her children will never again see each other. Don't you think they suffer as we would?"

"It's not the same! Slaves are not people; they're property. Remember that the United States Supreme Court said so!"

"I remember what William said about the Dred Scott decision. But I disagree, and so do most of the people in this country. At least in the North. I tell you, Julie, if I live a thousand years, I'll never forget that poor black mother pleading in vain not to be separated from her children! That's enough to make me want to grow up to be an abolitionist!"

"Emily!" Julie glanced around to make sure nobody had overheard. "Don't ever say that in this house! Why, William would turn you out so fast. . . ." She paused, her eyes widening in realization. "Oh, I'm sorry! Please forget I said that!"

★ ★

"It's all right. We both know you're right. That's why I've got to get to Richmond and then across the Union lines while everyone here is still on speaking terms."

Slowly, Julie nodded. "I never thought I'd say it, but you're probably right. I love you too much to have you hurt any more than you already have been."

"So you'll help me?"

"Reluctantly, yes. You'll need passes to get through our own pickets from here to Richmond. Mama could give you a letter to General Robert E. Lee or President Jefferson Davis. But I don't know if even they could issue a pass that would get you through to the North."

Emily mused, "I wonder how abolitionists get slaves from the South into the Union?"

"I don't know, but you mustn't talk about such awful people! You know how Papa and William feel about them."

"Yes, that's why Uncle Silas quit speaking or even writing to my father. He wasn't actually an abolitionist but did consider himself a sympathizer." Emily took a deep breath, remembering how the brothers had been before they split over slavery. "I miss the place where I grew up, so I'm going to get to Illinois any way I can. If I knew an abolitionist—"

"Even that wouldn't work!" Julie broke in. "No matter how angry Mama and William are with you, they would never let you travel alone to the capital at Richmond. It's too dangerous."

"Oh, I hadn't even thought about that! Now I've got to figure out how to do that, too."

"William and Mama agree that the war will certainly escalate now that we beat the Yankees at Manassas. It won't be over in ninety days like everyone said at first. It could last a long time—maybe even years."

"That's all the more reason I've got to get to Richmond as fast as possible," Emily said. "So it's time to ask her if she will give me a letter of introduction to General Lee."

★ ★

"What if she won't?"

"I think she and William will be glad to have me gone. Anyway, I'm going to Richmond one way or another, and hopefully, within the week!"

★　★　★　★　★

Most slaves who worked the fields from dawn to dusk would have envied Nat. As personal attendant to young Master William, he lived in the big house, where it was warm and comfortable. He didn't have a bed, but at least he slept on a soft pallet instead of a rustling excuse for bedding, a corn-shuck mattress. His pallet lay just in the second-story hallway outside William's room, where Nat was available at night if his master called. Instead of rough shoes that didn't fit and cast-off clothes, Nat wore those cast off by his master.

But the field hands would not have liked almost never being out of the master's sight for a moment, day or night. They would not have liked the sudden blows William habitually rained upon Nat for the slightest infraction of the rules, real or imagined. Most of all, they would not have liked having no free time, not even on Saturday night when field slaves held dances in the barn.

There, for a few hours, they could laugh or talk or get acquainted with one another as human beings. Nat's only freedom was to think, and he used every spare moment to plan his escape.

But for that he would need help to make contact with someone having details on how to escape on the Underground Railroad. It wasn't a real railroad at all, but a system whereby secret sympathetic white people helped slaves escape their plantations in a desperate bid for freedom. "Conductors" hid fugitives in many ways while transporting them, often in the dead of night, from one "station" to the next. At each one another "conductor" repeated the dangerous process.

Some slaves had reportedly reached a free state, but others

★　★

had been caught. They were always punished. Some had even been whipped to death by vengeful masters. Some slaves were sold.

Most of what Nat had heard about escaping had been learned at his first master's plantation. Thaddeus Whitman had been a benevolent master, even defying the law to teach Nat how to read and write. Nat had also heard from Whitman about other masters' slaves using grease with black pepper in running away.

That mixture supposedly stuck to the bottom of shoes or feet and confused pursuing hounds. Nat needed pepper and grease from the kitchen, which was in a separate building from the big house. But cooks and helpers slept in the kitchen, and one might betray him if he asked for or was seen taking the ingredients he needed.

Even after he had those, he could not run until he knew where in the swamp to hide until the local conductor picked him up. Nat wasn't afraid of the ghosts that were said to inhabit the swamp. But he feared the poisonous snakes and biting insects like mosquitoes and red bugs that could drive a person crazy. He also knew about the black bears and other big animals, but he was more concerned about getting lost and never finding his way out. He had heard about that happening to others.

Before Nat could risk the swamp, he had to see the boy at Darlington—the one who might be his brother Rufus. If it was, they could escape together.

But first, Nat had to trust someone, even though Uncle George had warned him that there were fellow slaves who would tell the master or mistress about a planned escape in exchange for some small reward.

In the darkness of the late July night, Nat reviewed his limited options. *Uncle George or Sarah must know more than they've said.* The old coachman had said he was too old to try

★ ★

running away. Still, he had guessed Nat's intentions and had not betrayed him.

Sarah had tried to escape with Pete, the man with the severely scarred back. The master seemed to think that Sarah might run again, which is why he made her wear the iron shackle that scarred her ankle.

Nat tried to decide whether Sarah could be trusted. She had told him where she and Pete had made their mistake in trying to escape to freedom and what they should have done instead.

Nat had not slept when he heard the faint cow horn sound from the slave quarters, rousing the field hands for another day even though it was not yet dawn. Nat sighed and made his decision.

First, I've got to find a way to get over to Darlington Plantation and see if Rufus is there. I may have to risk trusting George or Sarah to help me. I've got to hurry because if Sarah's right, the Underground Railroad will be leaving in a few days, and I have to be ready to go with it. But how do I make arrangements?

Nat got up, determined to take the necessary steps to carry out his dangerous plans.

★ ★ ★ ★ ★

Gideon opened his eyes to the dawn and the dense foliage of trees overhead. *So far, so good*, he told himself with satisfaction. *I guess I was wrong about Cobb or somebody following me.* He glanced beyond the smoldering campfire, where the boy who called himself Zeb had made a bed of leaves and boughs from trees.

Zeb was gone.

Alarmed, Gideon stood up and glanced around. He saw the boy running toward him from the direction where they had tied Hercules.

"What's the matter?" Gideon asked in alarm.

"Somebody done stole our mule!" Zeb panted.

★ ★

THE ROAD TO TROUBLE

The boys rushed to where Hercules had been picketed on a long rope. They found one end still tied to a tree trunk, but the other end had been cleanly cut as by a knife. The dragoon saddle and blanket were gone. A set of human footprints beside the mule's hoof marks showed that the thief had quietly led the animal toward the rural dirt road.

Indignation boiled within Gideon. "That Barley Cobb is about the meanest, low-down person in the world!"

"Who's he?"

"A slave catcher from near where I live. Yesterday I thought he was following me, but I never really saw him, so I decided it was just my imagination. Looks like it wasn't. Stealing Hercules means I can't do what needs to be done in the little time there is to . . . Wait!"

Gideon paused as a new thought struck him. "Why would Cobb steal the mule?"

"You just said he's the meanest—"

"He is," Gideon interrupted, "but there's something else. If he's the one following us, he's already riding a horse, so why would he want a mule?"

"That's easy: He wants us to walk."

Gideon pondered that. "That would be true if he wanted us to slow down. But . . ." He left his sentence unfinished as his mind raced ahead.

★ ★

Cobb doesn't know where Papa buried the gold, and he doesn't know I've got a map, so he could just ride ahead and wait for me to dig it up. Then he could try to steal it from me. The sooner I get to Manassas, the better for him, so he wouldn't have stolen Hercules.

"But what?" Zeb prompted.

Gideon delayed answering while his mind raced on. *Once I dig it up, Cobb would then have to take it from me. But he wouldn't want me to know it was him because I would turn him in to the law. So he must plan to rob me while I'm asleep, or maybe wear a mask and take it by force. So who did steal the mule, and why?*

Gideon replied to Zeb, "I can't say, except it's to Cobb's advantage that I don't lose Hercules."

"You ain't makin' sense, but if he didn't, who did?"

"I don't know, but let's see if we can find out anything from their tracks." Gideon was used to reading signs while hunting wild animals, so he followed the trail to the roadside where the thief had taken time to saddle the mule.

"Then he headed toward Manassas Junction," Gideon pointed out. "So he's going our way." Gideon felt a tinge of hope replace his anger and fear. "He's walking the mule slowly, probably to keep us from hearing him. Let's grab our stuff. Maybe we can catch up with him."

"Two boys on foot can't catch up to no mule!"

Gideon started running back toward the camp. "That's probably what he's figuring on, so he may not hurry."

"Or he may kick that old mule into a gallop as soon as he's out of earshot."

"Maybe, but no matter. I've got to get that mule back! Everything depends on it!"

Returning to camp, Gideon grabbed both the small cast-iron skillet and the little pan and dashed to the river for water to douse the fire. Then he quickly rolled his blankets and slung them over his back.

★ ★

THE ROAD TO TROUBLE

"Ain't we goin' to have breakfast?" Zeb protested.

"We can eat Mama's leftover corn bread on the way. Maybe you're in no hurry, but I am. So move if you're coming with me."

"Even if we'uns catch up to him," Zeb said as they returned to the road and headed toward Manassas, "how do you reckon on takin' that mule away from a growed man?"

"I don't know yet. First, let's catch up. . . ." Gideon paused as the first rays of the morning sun showed a small bag in the deep dust. He picked it up for a closer look and read the wording on the front. *B.D. Harwood, 1st Penn. Cav'y.*

Gideon turned to Zeb. "That answers the question about who stole Hercules: a Yankee cavalryman named Harwood from Pennsylvania." Gideon opened the drawstring and saw the contents were a stencil kit with brush, bottle, and ink. "Since he's alone, it probably means he's either a deserter or lost."

"Either way, he's likely got a rifle gun, too. Why don't we jist fergit 'bout catchin' up with him and jist figger it's safer to walk all the way?"

"No!" Gideon's voice was firm. He stuck the pouch in his pocket and broke into a jog, kicking up the dust from the deserted road. "You can do what you want, but I've got to get that mule back, and soon!"

"What if he sees you first and shoots you dead?"

"I'll be real careful, but I've got a responsibility for more than myself. You don't, so you had better stay here." Gideon increased his pace, leaving Zeb behind.

A moment later Zeb called, "Hey! Wait for me!"

The boys jogged on, their breakfast forgotten.

★ ★ ★ ★ ★

From where she was propped up in her canopy bed, Aunt Anna looked very frail from one of her frequent and unexplained sick "spells." She said, "Now, Emily, we've been over

★ ★
55

this before when my husband was still here. There's no use doing it again."

"It would be better for everyone if you helped me get home to Illinois!" Emily protested.

"Be realistic, my dear. Your entire family is dead and buried, so you have no home up North. Now your place is here with us at Briarstone."

Emily cast an imploring look at Julie, who shrugged, indicating it was useless for her to say anything. Emily turned back to her aunt. "Do you mind if I talk to William?"

"My son and I have already discussed this issue, my dear. We agree that it would be improper for us to let you leave."

"How would it be improper to give me a letter of introduction to General Lee? I could find a suitable woman traveling companion to go with—"

"You don't understand!" her aunt interrupted. "We're your only living relatives, so it would reflect adversely on my husband, son, and me to let you go all the way to Richmond in wartime. No, Emily. You must stay here."

"Are you saying that you're concerned because of what the neighbors would say if I left?"

"Well, of course, it's also our Christian duty. . . ."

Emily didn't hear any more. She was too polite to say it out loud, but she thought, *She's not the least bit concerned with me. Appearance is all she cares about.*

Emily forced herself to speak calmly. "I appreciate what all of you have done, but I don't want anything out of a sense of duty! Won't you and William please reconsider and give me that letter?"

Aunt Anna pressed both hands to her temples and began massaging them. "I'm getting a headache. You must excuse me."

Emily hesitated for a moment, then wordlessly turned and fled the room in total frustration.

★ ★

★　★　★　★　★

Gideon set a fast jogging pace that made the younger boy struggle to keep up.

Zeb protested in panting gasps, "You wouldn't stop so's we could eat that corn bread like civilized folks, an' you're nigh onto runnin' me to death. You seem bound and determined to catch up with that feller who stole our mule, even if it means getting us shot dead."

Gideon shot a look at Zeb, thinking, *Our mule?*

Zeb added, "So the least you kin do is tell me more than you have so far."

Gideon shaded his eyes with his hand and peered down the deserted road. "Still no sign of them."

"Don't try to change the subject!"

"I'm not; I'm just trying to figure out what to do if we catch up to that thief. In the meantime I've got to keep moving."

"Well, then, how 'bout tellin' me the whole blessed truth? You said you didn't run away from home like me, but why is a slave catcher chasin' you? You don't look like no runaway black boy to me. An' why air ye in sech a rush to git us shot at?"

Gideon grinned. "You ask a lot of questions."

"It's a long walk to Manassas, so ye kin take yore time an' tell me everything."

Gideon couldn't risk mentioning the buried gold. Zeb might tell someone before it could be recovered. Gideon also didn't feel comfortable saying that he wanted to see Emily before she left for Illinois. He had already spoken about his wounded half brother, but the story of how Gideon came to be riding the mule might satisfy Zeb.

He nodded. "All right. It all started when my father and I took a wagonload of wheat to Manassas Junction just before the soldiers had their big fight there."

Zeb's eyes opened wide in surprise. "You was thar?"

"We were actually at Centreville, about five, six miles past

★　★

Bull Run Creek and Manassas. We didn't mean to be. We sold our wheat, but before we could get away, a trainload of men and women from Washington City arrived to see the fight between their army and ours."

"I heard 'bout that but didn't rightly believe it. Womenfolks coming out to see men kill each other."

"It's true. Besides those on the cars, some came in fine carriages. They carried picnic baskets and were ready for a high old time. But they got fooled when our boys beat them so bad the Yankees panicked and ran over everybody trying to get back across the Potomac."

"Wish I seen that," Zeb said wistfully.

"It was something, all right, but terrible."

Both boys fell silent as they continued walking, kicking up dust from the road that continued toward Manassas.

Finally Zeb reminded Gideon, "You was a-gonna finish telling me things."

"Oh yes." Gideon glanced ahead, but there was no sign of the soldier who had stolen Hercules, although his hoofprints were still plain in the dust.

"Our wagon tipped over and I got knocked out. When I came to, one of our two mules was dead and the other so badly injured he couldn't live. My poor papa was about out of his mind with worry when a black man brought us two Yankee cavalry horses. They had blood on their saddles, so we knew they had run away when their riders didn't need them anymore. Papa and I jumped on them and rode for our lives up the Shenandoah Valley, then home. We gave one horse to Cobb because the mule that got killed belonged to him. Papa traded the other horse for Hercules because farmers like mules better than horses."

Zeb's eyes shone with excitement. "I want to see lots of fightin' and reckon I will when I jine up when we git to Manassas."

"I saw enough war to last me a lifetime." Gideon's voice dropped to a somber whisper. "I just want to see my brother and then get home. I sure hope my father's feeling better by—"

Gideon broke off his words and grabbed Zeb by the arm. "Look! There's Hercules!"

The boys stood in the deep dust, their eyes probing ahead. The saddled mule was tied to a wooden fence by a small stand of white pines, but there was no sign of the thief who had stolen him.

"Reckon it's a trap?" Zeb whispered, eyes sweeping the woods. "Maybe that so'jer's hidin' behind a tree with his big old rifle gun, waitin' fer us to git close enough to cut us down with a ball."

Slowly, Gideon shook his head. "I don't think so. Look over there by that log at the edge of the woods."

"I see him!" Zeb started to turn around to run away, but again Gideon grabbed him.

"Take another look; a real good look."

Reluctantly, tensed to dash off, the younger boy shaded his eyes and carefully scrutinized the blue-uniformed man. "A Yankee! He's tied up to that log! I kin see the ropes . . . wait! Maybe he's jist foolin', making out he's tied so's he can shoot us when we git closer."

"I don't think so. Look at his gun. It's broken in two, and he's struggling against the ropes where somebody tied him. He's mad as a wet hen, but he can't get free."

Cautiously, the boys approached. The cavalryman's uniform was dirty and torn, his cap was gone, and the midday sun had burned his forehead. He stopped struggling against his bonds and smiled as the boys came near.

"I'm mighty glad you two came along," he said. "Somebody bushwhacked me while my back was turned. Now, if you'll untie me . . ."

"That's our mule!" Zeb announced. "You stole him from us an' we want him back."

Surprise showed in the soldier's face. "There must be some mistake. I never saw you boys before in my life!"

★ ★

"That's probably true," Gideon agreed, producing the stencil bag. "I think this is yours, Mr. Harwood." From the startled look on his face, Gideon knew he was right. He tossed the pouch toward the thief. "We must have looked like just a couple of lumps under our blankets when you sneaked into our camp before dawn this morning."

"Now, boys, cut me loose and we'll talk this—"

Zeb broke in, turning to Gideon. "Let's leave him here for the varmints and git back on our mule."

Gideon felt a tinge of annoyance over Zeb's repeated references to "our" mule, but he agreed with the younger boy. "We walked enough, Mr. Harwood. Now it's your turn."

"Wait! If you won't untie me, at least throw that knife over where I can reach it."

"What knife?" Gideon asked in surprise, whirling to look where the man indicated with outthrust chin.

"Whoever snuck up on me and walloped me alongside the head used a pocketknife to cut off the piece of rope he tied me up with. He dropped it there on the ground out of my reach."

Gideon took a couple of steps and picked up the knife. Crude initials had been scratched in the handle.

" 'O.O.' " Gideon read softly, then his eyes opened wide. "What did he look like?"

"Oh, kinda short and stocky with hair like yours, only more reddish. Hadn't shaved in a long time."

"Oakley Odell!" Gideon muttered. "The patroller who works with Cobb!"

"What?" Zeb asked.

"Tell you later." Gideon looked back at Harwood. "What happened to your gun?"

"He smashed it against a tree and rode off on my horse. Both gun and horse belong to the Union."

He motioned with his chin to where Gideon saw the weapon with the stock broken off and the muzzle stuck into the dirt.

★ ★

Harwood continued. "He said that I could either drag this log over to my knife and cut myself free or become buzzard bait. I moved this broken log some but not enough. You boys gotta help me."

Gideon told Zeb, "This Yankee can't catch us if he's afoot, but we need a half hour or so head start. Maybe we could move the knife a little closer. What do you think?"

"That's too good for a blue belly," Zeb protested.

"No, boys! Cut me loose!" Harwood pleaded. "Some Rebel farmer may come along and use a pitchfork on me!"

"Rebel?" Gideon exclaimed, rankling at the derogatory term. "You invade our land when all we want to be is left alone! So don't call us Rebels!"

"Sorry," Harwood apologized. "But if you don't help me, I'll have sunstroke before this day is over!"

"We wouldn't want that, even if you are a thief," Gideon commented. "Say, Zeb, why don't you find his cap and put it on him while I throw what's left of the gun into the creek, just in case? Then let's ride out of here. We've lost enough time."

In moments, ignoring the thief's cries of protest, Gideon was again in Hercules' saddle, with Zeb riding behind. Hope again filled Gideon's heart as he urged the mule into a trot toward Manassas.

"Who's Oakley Odell?" Zeb asked.

"A no-good redneck who works with Barley Cobb."

"You reckon this Odell followed you yesterday?"

"I'm pretty sure of it." Gideon didn't think Odell was smart enough to plan anything like a robbery, but he could figure out that Gideon had to get to the gold and dig it up so it could be stolen. That kind of planning could only have been done by Cobb, who was smart in some devious ways. So Odell had to be following Cobb's orders. Gideon told Zeb, "When Odell realized our mule was gone, he rode ahead fast on his horse and fixed it so that we would get Hercules back. Odell wants us to get to Manassas real fast, but I can't tell you why."

★ ★

"If you're right, what happens when we get there?"

Gideon had a terrible feeling he knew the answer, but he couldn't tell Zeb about the gold. Even after he recovered it, how was he going to get it safely back to his family without it being forcibly taken from him?

That ominous threat lingered in Gideon's mind like the dust in the air from the mule's drumming hooves.

★ ★

LONG AFTER THE BATTLE

The boys rode hard, keeping the mule at such a steady pace that they started passing a few farmhouses before sunset. It was about that time that Gideon caught a whiff of such a terrible stench he almost gagged.

From where he rode behind Gideon, Zeb exclaimed, "Phew! What *is* that?"

Two ugly vultures and some ravens flapped heavily into the air from near a line of trees. Gideon replied, "Dead horse, I think."

"I see it now." As more scavengers took to the air, Zeb added, "There's another one over there. And two—no, three more. What do you suppose happened?"

Gideon's gaze skimmed the plains, taking in scattered bits of clothing, canteens, haversacks, and other items. "This must be part of the Manassas battlefield. There hasn't been time to bury or burn all the animals that got killed when we beat the Yankees."

Gideon felt the younger boy tighten his arms where he had been holding on to his waist. "You reckon some dead people are still out there, too?"

"I doubt it." Gideon tried to sound confident, but as dark shadows crept out of the trees and inched toward the riders, he wasn't sure.

"I ain't skeered of dead so'jers or nothin' like that," Zeb said

★ ★
63

with a little tremor in his voice, "but I sure wish we could find us a farmhouse where we could have a real light, an' not a campfire like last night."

Gideon didn't answer but tried to breathe as little as possible while peering intently ahead to where the line of trees curved to the right. "You smell smoke?" he asked, automatically sniffing before he thought. The foul air overtook the woodsmoke, turning his stomach.

"Sure do! Over thar!" Zeb thrust his left hand out toward where a second stand of trees stood on a small hill. "Farmhouse! Reckon maybe they'll let us sleep in their barn tonight?"

Gideon hesitated. He had lost time over the stolen mule, but it was too late to try locating the right landmarks to dig up the gold tonight. He couldn't do that with Zeb, so Gideon said, "Let's go ask." He pulled on the left rein and headed for the building.

What was left of shell-blasted shade trees stood like broken skeletons outside the frame structure. Twin brick chimneys rose into the evening sky at both ends of the two-story home. A second, smaller chimney marked the white wooden kitchen, which stood several feet from the big house. To the rear, a sturdy-looking barn looked inviting. But there were ugly, gaping holes in every building where musket balls or artillery shells had struck. Still, there was a comforting look to the place, although the offensive odor still assaulted their nostrils.

Gideon rode to the split-rail fence and dismounted, so stiff after hours in the saddle that he almost stumbled. There was no gate, but he walked up a wide set of stairs with four steps that led over the fence.

An attractive young woman with dark hair parted in the center and pulled back above her ears stepped out onto the front porch. She wiped her hands on an apron and thoughtfully studied the boys.

"Sorry to bother you," Gideon said, politely sweeping his

★ ★

felt hat from his head and trying to smile in a friendly way, "but we're on our way to see my brother who got wounded at Manassas Junction, and we'd be mighty pleased if you let us sleep in the barn tonight."

She was about Isham's age and pretty, Gideon thought as she shifted her examination from him to Zeb.

He spoke quickly. "We'uns will stay one night only, and we won't be no bother. We'll be mighty keerful an' won't need nothin' but some well water for us and our mule. We got our own vittles, an' we won't even need a fire to cook. We kin eat cold food."

Gideon agreed. "That's right. We'll be gone before sunup so I can find my brother."

"Very well," the woman decided. "I would invite you in, but this place was suddenly turned into a hospital during the battle. We still have some soldiers too wounded to move, so there's no room except the barn."

"Suits us fine," Gideon replied, smiling with relief. "Oh, before we go, how much farther is it to Camp Pickens? That's where my brother was, last we knew."

"Not far. You'll get there easily tomorrow morning." The woman started to turn back toward the front door but stopped. "What're your names?"

"Tugwell; Gideon Tugwell, from near Church Creek."

"I'm Zeb," the younger boy said. "It's really Zebulun, but I answer to Zeb. Zeb Trotter, late of the Blue Ridge Mountains."

The woman's attention suddenly focused on Gideon. "Tugwell?"

"Yes'm. I'm named after my father. Some folks call him 'Old Gideon' and me 'Young Gid—"

"What's your brother's name?" the girl interrupted.

"He's really my half brother who was wounded. His name is Isham."

"It is?" When Gideon nodded, she made rapid motions for

him to approach her. "Come in! Come in! There's someone I'd like you to see."

★ ★ ★ ★ ★

Emily and Julie wandered in thoughtful silence under the great shade trees lining the long driveway from the public road to Briarstone's manor house.

A flock of geese waddling arrogantly along in an irregular gray parade suddenly broke into raucous honking. Both girls turned to see a horse pulling a covered four-wheeled carriage with the side shades drawn. The driver slowed for the turn into the driveway.

"I recognize the coachman," Julie said. "He's from Darlington. But I can't see who's inside because the curtains are down. Oh, I hope it's not bad news!"

Emily had never been to the neighboring plantation, but she had heard about the Cummings family who lived there. They had a son in his early twenties who had joined the Confederate artillery the day after Lincoln called up Union militia men to serve ninety days.

That period had now passed, and the war wasn't over as both North and South had expected it would be. After the Federal defeat at Manassas Junction, both sides knew that the struggle would continue for a long time.

The black reinsman brought the horse to a stop beside the girls. Julie looked expectantly at him. He showed white teeth in a smile of greeting but didn't speak. He just glanced at the closed curtains.

Both girls followed his eyes as the near side curtain was suddenly lifted and a curly-haired young man in gray uniform grinned at them. "Guess who's back?" he cried, dropping the curtain and shoving the door open without waiting for the coachman to do it.

"Theodore!" Julie cried happily, reaching both hands out to him as he stepped out. "When did you get home?"

★ ★

"Late last night. I've only got three days' furlough, but I'm very pleased to have them." He shifted his gray eyes to Emily. "You must be the Yankee girl everyone's talking about. I'm your neighbor Theodore Cummings, from Darlington."

"How do you do?" she replied formally. "I'm Emily Lodge, Julie's cousin from Illinois."

"I am honored to know you, Miss Emily." He gave a slight bow and grinned in a way that reminded her of the way Brice Barlow had teased her back home in happier times.

He was of average height, five feet eight inches tall, with a boyish look around the eyes and mouth. Emily decided that he was quite nice looking, although not as handsome as Brice.

"Ladies," Theodore continued, turning to reach inside the coach's semidarkened interior, "I brought someone special with me."

He reached inside to take hold of a slender white hand with long, tapered fingers. An attractive woman in her late teens emerged smiling to stand beside him.

"Annabelle!" Julie exclaimed, stepping into the open arms extended to her. "How good to see you again!" Emily found herself smiling in spite of her personal problems. It was obvious that the newly arrived couple was special to Julie.

Annabelle released Julie and turned to Emily. "I'm Annabelle Harper. I have heard so much about you." She extended her right hand to Emily, who felt the softness of those graceful long fingers, which obviously had never done any housework.

Emily gave a slight curtsy as Annabelle smiled warmly and confessed, "I must say you're much less fearful looking than I had been led to believe by some of the older people around this area."

It was meant as humor, Emily knew, but she was also keenly aware that there was some question about her loyalty in the minds of other planters.

Theodore seemed to sense Emily's discomfort, for he quickly changed the subject. "This war has already destroyed

★ ★

some of our more cherished customs," he began, smiling again. "There is no time to be formal and have Annabelle's parents send the proper invitations around on a silver tray, so Annabelle and I have come to personally extend an invitation to our wedding."

"Wedding?" Julie almost squealed with delight. "Oh, I've been expecting to hear that for the last couple of years! When is the happy day?"

"This Saturday at sunset," the couple replied together, exchanging slightly embarrassed glances.

Theodore added, "We would like to make it sooner because I have such little time before I have to report back for duty, but Annabelle wants a formal wedding. Fortunately, she has been planning it for months."

"Actually," Annabelle said softly, lowering her eyes, "we became betrothed before Theodore joined up, but we kept it secret from all but our families in hopes we could announce it more formally when the war was over. But after Manassas . . ." Her voice ended on a sad note.

"What she's trying to say," her fiancé explained, "is that since that battle, it's obviously not going to be a short war as everyone expected. So we're going to be married before I report back, and you're both invited to the wedding."

"Oh!" Julie clapped her hands like a little girl. "Thank you! We'll be there, won't we, Emily?"

Emily hesitated. Her cousin had momentarily forgotten about Emily's hopes to leave for Richmond by then.

"Wonderful!" Theodore exclaimed. "Naturally, Julie, the invitation extends to your mother and brother, too. Please beg their forgiveness because Annabelle and I can't take the time to extend the invitation to them personally. But we have other neighbors we must see as soon as possible while our parents do the same."

When the carriage had gone, Julie gave Emily a quick, impulsive hug. "Oh, it's going to be a most wonderful wedding.

★ ★

There won't be any men except old ones, and young boys. All the others are off to the war. But you'll enjoy meeting other planters from the area, plus families from church, the village, and miles around!"

Julie grabbed Emily's hand and gave it a tug. "Come on! Let's go decide what to wear!"

The cousins started running back toward the big house before Emily cried in dismay, "Oh, Julie! I can't! I hope to be headed for Richmond by then."

"There's no chance of that. Come on."

Reluctantly, Emily felt that was true, so she followed Julie into the house, where she was already calling for Toby, her personal servant. At the same moment Emily thought of something that gave her a glimmer of hope. Maybe she would meet someone at the wedding who would accompany her to the capital. If she had that done, there might be a chance that William and Aunt Anna would change their minds and let her go.

Emily said, "Julie, attending this wedding could be very exciting!"

★　★　★　★　★

It had always been a source of amusement to Nat and other slaves that they heard most things newsworthy even before the masters or mistresses did. So Nat merely nodded and replied as expected when William instructed him to get his dark suit ready for a wedding. "Yessuh, Massa," Nat replied in the slave dialect that was expected of even the household servants. *I'll be ready, too.*

He had decided that during the few minutes after the girls had rushed breathlessly into the house with news of the wedding. Nat was required to attend William wherever he went. At Darlington that would give Nat two opportunities that he desperately needed.

While he and Uncle George waited for the white folks to complete their evening of celebration, Nat must somehow get a look at the new slave boy who might be his brother. Even if he was, it would be difficult to talk privately with Rufus and persuade him to join in escaping to freedom. That is, if he could learn when and how to start on the Underground Railroad and if there would be room for him and his brother.

So far, he had not learned anything more from George or Sarah because there had been no way to talk privately. While he waited for that opportunity, he had to be sure whether Rufus was at Darlington. William always took Nat on social outings, so while the wedding celebration was going on, he would have to slip off and look for Rufus. If he got caught, he would face more than a whipping and possibly being sent down the river. His burning desire in life would be extinguished, and he might as well be dead. So he must not fail. With that assurance he went to the young master's bedchamber to prepare for Saturday night.

★　★　★　★　★

The smell inside the farmhouse was worse than it had been outside. The reason was obvious. Gideon remembered the awful stench when his uncle died of gangrene from a deep cut in his leg.

When the young woman led Gideon and Zeb past two open bedroom doors on the ground floor, Gideon glimpsed a pale young man lying on the high bed with a bandaged stump of a right leg. In the other room a sandy-haired youth had only one foot. Gideon suspected they would soon die.

"I forgot to introduce myself," their teenage guide said as she led Gideon and Zeb up a flight of stairs. "I'm Carolyn Adams. My parents and I live here. It was always such a peaceful place until that awful battle. I'm sorry you boys have to see what war is like." She turned to Zeb. "Are you two related?"

"No, ma'am. We jist met a spell back."

"I see." On the second floor she paused outside the first open door on the right and knocked on the sill.

★　★

"Come in," a male voice called softly.

Carolyn stuck her head in the door. "Would you like a visitor?"

Gideon couldn't hear the answer, but Carolyn turned to him and Zeb and motioned for them to enter. Feeling very ill at ease and bewildered, they stepped inside and stopped. A silent figure on the high poster bed had his right arm in a sling and a bandage around his head.

"Isham," Carolyn said, gently pushing Gideon forward, "I believe you know this young man."

"Isham?" Gideon repeated in surprise and took another look. "It is you!" Rushing toward the bed, Gideon started to throw his arms around his half brother, but Carolyn's voice stopped him.

"Gideon! Careful of his arm!"

The boy stopped, his eyes widening at the sight of the bandage that extended from shoulder to elbow.

Isham let out a whoop of surprise and joy. "Gideon! Don't pay any attention to her! Come here and let me give you a big bear hug!"

Carefully, but with enthusiasm, Gideon obeyed. His brother's good left arm encircled him and pulled him off his feet so he sprawled across Isham's chest.

For the better part of a minute, they stayed that way while Isham tried to speak, but his voice broke and he stifled a sob. Gideon blinked back the hot mist that suddenly clouded his eyes.

He heard Carolyn's voice from the foot of the bed. "Zeb, let's leave them alone. I made a pie today. Would it spoil your supper to eat a little piece now?"

"No, ma'am. It shore won't hurt my appetite none."

She gave Gideon and Isham a quick smile, then led Zeb down the hall toward the stairs.

Gideon motioned to Isham's arm. "How bad is it?"

"A blue belly put a musket ball in it. Missed the bone, but

it's not healing well. Fact is, the doctor wanted to cut it off, but I saw what happened to the others when he sawed off an arm or leg. Several died."

"Oh, Isham! You're not going to—?"

"Not if I can help it," his brother said quickly with a wry smile. "I want to get back to our farm someday."

Gideon remembered his uncle, but he didn't think Isham's wound smelled like gangrene.

"Now," Isham said, patting the bed with his good hand, "hop up here and tell me about the family and why you're here."

Isham had enough problems of his own, but Gideon steeled himself to tell the bad news he carried.

RISK LEADS TO DANGER

Gideon leaned back on his brother's bed and sighed. He had not told Isham about wanting to get back to Church Creek in time to see Emily before she left for the North, but he had left nothing else out. He said, "So that's why I'm here."

"You'd better close the door," Isham suggested. "We have to work out your problems so you can get home safely."

Gideon slid off the bed to approach the door. "I wish you could go with me."

"So do I. I've put in for a furlough to recover at home, but so far the doctor won't let me." With the door closed Isham lowered his voice. "You're sure carrying a lot of responsibility for your age. Isn't this the first time you've been away from home alone?"

"Yes, it is."

"Now you have to find the gold so Papa's doctor bills can be paid and the family has something to live on this winter. Yet Odell apparently is following you, probably to steal the gold when you dig it up."

"Cobb must have told him about the gold because he's the one who overheard Lilly mention that Papa had buried it on our last trip."

"Oh, I think Cobb is behind it, but he's probably trying to keep that secret. Later, he can claim to be innocent so he can still live around Church Creek with decent folks. He may have hired Odell without telling him about the gold, or maybe he offered to split it with him after Odell stole it. At any rate, this is all too much for you to handle alone."

"I found you, so I can tell the folks I did that part right, and I can get the gold safely home, too."

"I'm proud of you, little brother, but you still need help." Isham scowled. "When the surgeon comes tomorrow, I'm going to ask again for a medical leave so I can help you with the gold and then see you safely home. If Odell tries to rob us, I can shoot with my good hand if necessary."

"I'd sure like to have you along, but why would the doctor change his mind even if you ask again?"

"Because I'll push hard, and if he won't agree, I may have to go anyway."

"No! That's desertion! I've heard they shoot soldiers who do that!"

"I know, but your life could be in danger, too."

"You really think Odell would. . . ?"

"I hope not, but he's a wild one, so I don't want you to risk getting hurt, or worse. Tomorrow I'll go with you to recover the gold."

Gideon hesitated, torn between the overwhelming desire to have his big brother's help and the nagging fear that Isham might lose his arm or even his life if he didn't stay under the doctor's care.

While the boy struggled with a decision, his brother also fell silent. The only sound was from the ground floor where one of the wounded soldiers moaned. They had all suffered leg or foot wounds or were otherwise unable to climb stairs.

Isham finally said sadly, "It's bad enough that older men have to fight battles, but it's hard for those your age to see what war really does. It's going to get worse, too. So it isn't all honor and glory as they say in speeches."

Gideon was heartsick at what little he had seen of war, but he didn't want to let his brother know how worried he was about him. Gideon changed the subject. "How come you're here instead of a hospital?"

"After the battle at Manassas, the wounded were taken wherever they could be treated. In my case, I was shot and fell into heavy brush along Bull Run Creek. I hit my head on a tree and was knocked cold. I wasn't found until the next day."

Gideon closed his eyes, aware of both the physical and mental pain Isham must have suffered during those long hours.

"Carolyn's father finally found me," Isham added. "This farm is on the edge of the fifteen hundred acres where the battle was. He heard me moaning while he was out in his field. I was so weak from loss of blood that I barely remember him coming, going away, and then returning with a wagon and Carolyn to help move me. They took me into their home, same as they had the others you saw; plus some who have since died. I'm mighty grateful to be alive."

"Me too."

"Enough about me," Isham said, his voice taking on a firm tone. "Are you still trying to write stories?"

"Yes, when there's time. Remember when you told me before leaving home that there was plenty to write about all around me if I'd just pay attention?"

"That's when I also told you to keep a journal. Are you doing that?"

"Not every day, but pretty often. Someday all those notes should help me write good stories."

"Don't forget to write what you saw here."

With a heavy sigh Gideon assured him, "I brought paper and a pencil to do that."

"Good! Now, let's talk about how to outsmart Odell so we can dig up that gold and get it home fast."

"I've been thinking about that, and I've got an idea."

"Oh?" Isham said. "Let's hear it."

★　★　★　★　★

★　★

Julie held her closet door open for Emily and motioned to the various fine outfits hanging there. "Pick one of mine and try it on. Toby can alter it so well that nobody at the wedding will guess it wasn't made especially for you."

Impulsively, Emily hugged her cousin. "You're so good to me! I feel guilty about even wanting to leave, but I just have to. You do understand, don't you?"

"I'm trying. Now, make your choice and get ready for a lot of fun."

Emily ran her eyes along the dresses with their wide hoop-skirts while imagining how each would look on her. She critically eyed a blue taffeta before asking, "Who's going to be there?"

"Absolutely everybody. Mostly planters and their families, of course, plus some people from the village. That will surely include Mr. and Mrs. Yates. Everyone invites them even though their newspaper opposed having Virginia secede from the Union. Most planters are convinced the Yateses are abolitionists, although nobody can prove that."

Emily forgot about the garments. She turned to face her cousin. "What do you think?"

"I don't really know, but Papa always thought so, and of course Mama and William do. Before Papa left for the war, he said that Mr. and Mrs. Yates manumitted the slaves they inherited."

"Manumitted?" Emily repeated.

"Freed them from slavery. Their former servants now work for them on wages, as freedmen."

"Then why do people invite the Yateses if they are suspected of being abolitionists?"

"Papa said the Yateses' ancestors were here even before most of the planters. They're well off financially and they own the local newspaper, plus a farm. I also think people are a little afraid of Mrs. Yates."

★ ★

"Afraid of her?" Emily asked, her mind spinning with ideas. "Why is that?"

"I'm not quite sure. She really runs the newspaper because her husband likes to grow fruit trees on some acreage they own. She never threatens or anything, and he is quiet as a mouse. But Papa says that the Yateses are very strong-minded people, and not the kind you want to cross."

Emily thoughtfully nodded and turned back to lift the blue taffeta from the closet. "How about this one?"

"That would have been my choice for you. Try it on." She stepped to the door and opened it. "Toby, come in here."

Emily stood quietly after slipping into the garment. The slave girl expertly examined it, giving it a tug here and there. Emily remained silent, her mind racing. *I've got to meet Mrs. Yates Saturday night*, she decided, *but I can't tell Julie because I don't want her to be involved and get her in trouble. But maybe Mrs. Yates can help me get to Richmond.*

★ ★ ★ ★ ★

Obeying his young master's next order to have George wash and polish the coach, Nat entered the carriage house where the old driver was repairing a halter. Nat relayed the message, then turned to leave but stopped at the old man's soft word.

"Wait."

The slave boy turned back to the gray-haired reinsman. "Yes?"

"That girl Sarah. She told me that she needs to speak to you privately when you get a chance."

Nat's brow furrowed in thought. "Why does she want to see me?"

George shrugged and replaced the halter on a wall peg. "She didn't say, but I can guess."

"Then guess."

The driver's brown eyes probed the area to make sure nobody was close enough to hear. Even so, he lowered his voice

★ ★

to barely a whisper. "I think she might have some thoughts on where and when a 'conductor' plans to pick up some 'passengers' for the next train ride, if you know what I mean."

Nat knew. "I've got to get back before William wants me for something. But if I could get away for a few minutes, where would I find Sarah?"

"She recently was moved from field hand to help Aunt Hattie in the kitchen. I saw Sarah going from there toward the smokehouse not two minutes ago. You could walk by there on your way back to the big house."

Nat nodded his thanks and hurried out into the darkness, guided toward the smokehouse by the pleasant fragrance of hams and other meats hanging there for curing. He was surprised to see that the door was not padlocked as usual for protection against stealing.

The door was slightly open, but there was no light inside. He couldn't imagine that a girl from the quarters would have a key that usually only the cook carried. Still, Nat approached, glancing cautiously around, not wanting anyone to see him in an area where he did not belong. He remembered how George had cautioned him not to trust anyone, for sometimes even another slave might report him to the master in hopes of some small reward.

As Nat paused outside the smokehouse door, he heard a faint clink of metal from Sarah's ankle shackle. Her voice followed. "Don't come in. Just tie your shoe or something in case anyone's watching. If someone comes along, start whistling."

Wordlessly, Nat bent over his shoe.

Sarah's voice was soft as the night air. "Young master sent word for me to 'marry.' "

"You know slaves can't—"

"Don't talk!"

Slaves couldn't legally marry. What Sarah meant was that she had reached child-bearing age, so the master had chosen a "husband" for her so she could produce offspring. Each child born on the plantation cost the master nothing but would grow up to be worth money to him.

Sarah whispered, "I'm not going to do it."

"You'll get whipped—"

"I said don't talk! George told me about you. Do you really want to cross over Jordan?"

Nat understood that she referred to a spiritual the slaves sang about crossing over the River Jordan. But it really was a symbol for the Potomac River and freedom. "Yes." Nat's reply was so low that he wasn't sure she heard him until she spoke again.

"In a few days a special farm wagon will pass by the swamp where the wooden bridge is. If a person was hiding nearby, he could slide into a hidden place under the wagon. It goes to Richmond on the way over Jordan."

Sarah fell silent, tempting Nat to ask, "What day, what time?" but a footstep behind startled him. He tried to whistle a warning, but sudden fear dried his lips. He puckered but couldn't whistle a note. All he could do was make a sound of air rushing through his lips, but that was apparently enough to warn Sarah.

Aunt Hattie, the black cook, waddled toward him, her bulk making a recognizable silhouette against the faint lamplights from the house. Nat sucked in his breath, fearful that she had come to get some meat from the smokehouse.

A top-notch cook for the master and mistress was often the most powerful member in a plantation's slave hierarchy. Hattie enjoyed that status and exercised her superior rights.

Spotting the young master's body servant, she asked suspiciously, "Whatcha all a-doin' out heah?"

Assuming the negro dialect expected of all slaves, Nat replied, "Jis a-fixin' muh shoe. Come untied."

"Y'all better git inside a-fore young massa catches you hangin' aroun' dis smokehouse."

"I will, sho' 'nuf."

★ ★

Still he hesitated, holding his breath while the heavy woman stopped in front of the smokehouse door and felt in her apron pocket. "I done fo'got muh key," she muttered. "Now, boy, go 'long wif ye."

Nat had no choice but to walk toward the big house. He glanced around to see the cook waddling back the way she had come. Nat switched his gaze to the smokehouse in time to see a slight, dark figure dart out of the door, bend low behind the English box hedges, and run toward the kitchen.

Nat continued toward the big house, his mind taunting him with two questions: *What day? What time?*

★ ★ ★ ★ ★

Gideon was pleased that his plan met with his older brother's reluctant approval. There was some risk to it, but they agreed that Odell probably would not expect Gideon to try recovering the gold that night.

After supper with Carolyn and her father, and while Zeb visited with Isham, Gideon followed Mr. Adams to the barn, where he provided the boy with a small piece of tin and a coal-oil lantern. He was grateful that the farmer asked no questions, even when Gideon fashioned the tin around the lantern so that it made only a small spot of light instead of shining in every direction.

Then, a little scared at what he was about to do all alone, Gideon mounted Hercules, carrying the unlit lantern and a shovel. Avoiding the road in case it was being watched, Gideon guided the mule through the night and across the fields before intersecting the road as Mr. Adams had suggested.

Still cautious, Gideon remained alert in case he and Isham were wrong and Odell did follow. Twice Gideon dismounted and circled back on his own trail to make sure there was no sign of anyone else on the road.

Feeling a little more sure of himself, Gideon entered Centreville. The dirt streets of the small community were deserted. Lamps showed in the windows of scattered one-story frame buildings. Gideon intersected the railroad tracks and followed them toward the train station. It was his first landmark remembered from the day his father's wagon tipped over and Gideon was knocked unconscious at the battle of Manassas.

The defeated Yankees had fled in panic from Bull Run Creek through Centreville, trampling women and men who had come from Washington to watch the fight.

Before leaving the farm Gideon had carefully studied the map his father had drawn. Now he visually recalled its details and looked for other landmarks.

Over there, he thought. *I'm sure that's where I got hurt. The stand of trees should be just past there.*

He squatted down so that the line of trees would be silhouetted against the skyline. For a full minute he stared into the night. Then he frowned.

Something's wrong! he realized. *This is the right place, all right. But where are the trees?*

With trembling fingers he struck a match and lit the lantern. He flashed the narrow beam around and groaned in despair.

Not a single tree remained! There was nothing but freshly cut stumps!

Oh no! How will I ever find the gold now?

★ ★

SHADOW OF A STRANGER

Gideon was panic-stricken and lost no time in returning to the farmhouse to report to Isham. "There's nothing left but stumps," the boy emphasized as he finished telling what he had found. "Stumps all look alike, so how can I find where Papa buried the gold?"

"Keep your voice down," Isham urged, even though the bedchamber door was closed. "There's got to be a way. Besides, I should have gone with you!"

"And risk making your wound worse?" Gideon shook his head. "Anyway, we're wasting time talking. What we have to do now is figure a way to find where Papa buried that gold and get back to him real fast."

"You're right." Isham reached out with his good hand and ruffled his little brother's hair. "I just don't want anything to happen to you."

"Me either. So let's think how to find the right place to dig up that gold."

"All right." Isham leaned back, easing his injured arm around carefully but still wincing with pain. "What kind of trees stood there when you and Papa saw them?"

"I didn't really pay much attention, but mostly cedar, maybe some pitch pine and Virginia pine—why?"

"Papa said he buried those double eagles under a white pine tree, right?" When Gideon nodded, Isham continued. "We don't necessarily need the standing trees. Do you remember what white pine bark, cones, and needles look like?"

"Sure. Most of the bark is smooth, the cones are long and don't have any prickles. The needles grow in groups of five. In fact, there are no other pines like that in Virginia."

Grinning, Isham said admiringly, "You'll make a writer because you notice things that most people don't."

"So what you're saying is that all we have to do is check around the tree stumps until we find one with smooth bark and white pinecones and needles around it. But what if there were lots of such trees in that stand?"

"It hasn't been very long ago, so we'll also look for freshly turned dirt."

Gideon looked doubtful. "What if Papa covered that up with leaves or branches or something?"

"He probably did, but the ground will still be soft. We'll poke a stick or something in every possible place."

"Not 'we'! You can't go! If you do anything to make your wound worse—"

"Wait! Wait!" Isham broke in. "You're sounding a lot like Papa or Mama! I'll ask the surgeon. If he won't let me go, then you have to take someone—maybe Carolyn's father. I trust him."

Gideon grinned. "Are you sweet on Carolyn?"

"All of us wounded are, but that's beside the point. We've got to recover that gold right away, and you've got to have some protection doing it. So if Mr. Adams will go along—"

"I'd rather take Zeb," Gideon interrupted. "I won't tell him about the gold, but if we get in trouble, we're both young and fast. We can run away."

"You'll have to tell him something without lying."

"That could be a problem."

"In the meantime, let's take another look at that map. Maybe Papa drew in some other landmarks that might help you in daylight."

★ ★

The door burst open and Zeb rushed in, eyes bright with excitement. "Guess what? Carolyn done says she knows a cap'n at Camp Pickens who jist might need a drummer! She's goin' to innerduce me tomorrow so maybe I can git the job!"

"That's great!" Gideon exclaimed. "I hope you get it." Silently, he added, *And I hope we find the right tree stump and get that gold tomorrow. This delay is making me nervous.*

★　★　★　★　★

Emily found herself caught up in the excitement of going to the wedding of Theodore and Annabelle. It wasn't just the idea of a festive atmosphere that delighted her but the prospect of talking to Clara Yates.

If Emily could talk to her alone, she might be able to find a female traveling companion for a trip to Richmond. Of course, Emily still would have to convince Aunt Anna and William to change their minds about her leaving, but that would have to wait.

Julie had loaned Emily one of her dresses that could be altered, but Julie was distressed because she had worn all her gowns before. There was no time to have Toby make a suitable new one, as would have been customary. The girls were now considering ways to alter the blue taffeta dress Emily had chosen and modify one of Julie's green silk garments so it would look new.

By lamplight in Julie's room, Toby stood silently by while the girls pored over the latest issue of *Godey's Lady's Book*, an authority on fashionable styles.

Emily pointed to one of the drawings in the publication. "How about those lace ruffles? If they were sewn on my sleeves and down the outside of my skirt . . ."

"Of course!" Julie said excitedly. "And Toby could add pleated ruffles at the bottom so it will look brand-new. I like it."

"Sounds good," Emily replied. "Oh, how about having a

couple of flowered ribbons falling from the waist to the floor like these?" She tapped the page. "They would look graceful if we're allowed to join in the dancing."

"Oh, they'll let us dance! There won't be as many men because they've gone off to fight the Yankees, but that's all the more reason why everyone who comes will be invited onto the floor, including people our age."

"At home," Emily said with a hint of sadness to her tone, "we didn't do much dancing, so I'm not very good at it."

"You won't have any trouble. Most are line dances like the Virginia Reel. You ever do that?"

"No, but I've seen it. Isn't that where two lines of couples start out facing each other?"

"That's it. Then all the couples take turns doing a series of figures. It's easy."

"But if there aren't enough men or boys our age, we might end up as wallflowers and be embarrassed."

"William's going to be there, so all of his friends will be, too. They'll ask us to dance."

"I'm not sure he would approve of them asking a suspected Yankee spy to be their partner," Emily said doubtfully.

"On the contrary! You'll be a lady of mystery. I can just hear them whispering now, both boys and girls." Julie lowered her voice and spoke from behind her hand. "Is she a spy or isn't she? Is she really an abolitionist? What does she think of the war?"

Returning to her normal tone, Julie added, "Those kinds of questions will make the boys want to talk to you. They will whether my brother likes it or not."

"You really think so?" Emily asked hopefully.

"No doubt in my mind. I just hope my brother doesn't make a scene."

"Over me?"

"No, I didn't meant that. He's more likely to get into an argument with someone about the best way to handle servants.

★ ★

You see, William doesn't think much of the Cummings family, except Theodore. They always got along, but William says Theodore's father, Homer, is too liberal with his servants. He doesn't believe in harsh punishments as my brother does."

Emily shook her long curls, thinking of the brutal whipping William had given the runaway slave the day before.

"But," Julie continued, "William will go because he's old enough to be thinking about girls, and every one of them for miles around will be there."

"Maybe William won't approve of us dancing."

"He won't even notice as long as we don't embarrass him." Julie picked up a pale green silk dress from several carefully laid on chairs around the room. "I think I'll wear this one after Toby adds some flounces. What do you think, Emily?"

Smiling, she said, "Without a doubt, you'll be the belle of the ball."

"I wish that were true." Julie sighed softly. "But I'll never be as pretty as you."

"Don't say things like that! You're going to be a lovely woman and make some man very happy."

"You think so?" Julie sounded wistful.

"Of course. Hold that dress against yourself and look in the mirror."

Julie did as instructed, then smiled. "It does make me look pretty."

"That's because you are, inside and out."

Still holding the garment against her, Julie gave a couple of happy whirls around the large bedchamber. "Oh, Emily! I'm so excited! This is going to be the first social gathering I've attended since the war. . . ."

A knock at the door caused Julie to stop in the middle of her pivoting. "Come in."

William stuck his head in the door. "Will you two be ready when the carriage leaves for the wedding Saturday night? I don't want to be late."

★ ★

"We'll be ready," Julie replied. "Have you got a minute to look at the gowns Emily and I are wearing?"

"I've got more important things to do," he mumbled and started to close the door.

"Just a minute, please," Emily said, hurrying toward him. "May I speak to you?"

He waited for her to step into the hallway and close the door before saying, "If it's about your leaving here for Illinois, save your breath."

Emily tried to ignore the discouragement that raced through her. "I appreciate all you and Aunt Anna have done for me," she began, "but I really want to return home."

William started down the hallway toward the top of the stairs. "You've said all that before, and my mother and I have answered you."

Hurrying to catch up to him, Emily tried again. "But if I had an adult traveling companion from here to Richmond, then would you reconsider. . . ?"

"No!" He stopped abruptly and faced her, his face flushed. "My mother also gave you an answer to that. Face it, Emily: You're going to stay here, *if* you behave yourself!"

He turned on his heel and clumped noisily down the stairs, leaving her standing awkwardly in the upstairs hallway. For a moment Emily remained still, feeling her speeding heartbeat against her temples.

He's so unreasonable! she thought, controlling her anger.

An idea snapped into her mind so suddenly that she jerked involuntarily. *Of course!* she told herself, her spirits rising. *That's his weakness, and I think I know how to use it to get him to change his mind!*

★ ★ ★ ★ ★

Nat carried a lantern down to the carriage house, where Uncle George sat outside the door alone, smoking his corncob pipe.

★ ★

Nat explained, "William sent me to remind you that he wants the best carriage washed and polished just before he leaves for the wedding."

"Already planned on that," the old reinsman replied, removing the pipe from his mouth and waving the stem in the air. "Won't be a speck of dirt on the carriage, the team, or me, 'cepting what the road throws up on the way over there."

"I rather expected you'd say that." Nat started to walk back toward the big house, but George's soft voice stopped him.

"Got a message for you." The words were so low that Nat barely heard them.

He glanced around, saw nobody near, and took a couple of steps closer to the driver. "Oh?"

Again, George's voice was barely audible. "Shortly after sunup next Monday."

Nat frowned, not understanding. He waited.

"Something else, too." George replaced the pipe in his mouth and puffed a couple of times. The whites of his eyes showed in the lantern light as he probed the shadows to make sure there were no other ears close by.

"Yes?" Nat prompted.

"Cobb, the slave catcher, has been gone someplace for a day or two, but now he's back." George's tone was so low that Nat had to bend forward to hear them.

Understanding started seeping into Nat's brain.

George continued in a low tone. "But a no-good white man name of Odell who sometimes works with him is still gone. The pattyrollers are always around, so be mighty careful."

The old coachman's uncanny way of seeming to know what Nat was thinking overwhelmed him. *He knows I'm going to run, and Sarah sent this message about the Underground Railroad through George, so she must trust him. That means he must trust me.*

The gray-haired coachman slowly got to his feet, knocked the remains of his pipe bowl into the dirt, and used his shoe

★ ★

to cover it. He whispered, "Only room for two on that trip over Jordan."

That news startled Nat. Sarah also planned to escape, and the "railroad" would have room for two: Nat and her. *But what about my brother?* Nat asked himself in sudden alarm. *If Rufus is at the next plantation and wants to go with me . . . well, there won't be room for three of us!*

Nat's thoughts tumbled over each other in rapid succession. Would Sarah really dare run again after she had unsuccessfully tried to escape when the old master was still home? She still wore the shackle on her ankle and carried punishment scars even though they were not as terrible as those suffered by Pete, who had tried escaping with her. But if she planned to run, did Nat even have the right to bring along his brother— if he turned out to be Rufus?

George's voice interrupted Nat's racing mind. "Y'all tell young Massa William duh carriage, it be ready," George said in slave dialect, his words loud enough so that anyone nearby could hear them. He walked inside to his living quarters.

Nat returned to the big house, his mind spinning. He had both a time and a place to meet the "conductor" of the secret Underground Railroad. But he also had big, unexpected complications plus a suddenly tight deadline to find out about his brother and be ready to flee.

★ ★ ★ ★ ★

Day had barely broken when Gideon rode alone down a deserted side street in Centreville. On one side of the slightly sloping dirt road, the boy saw only two white frame houses, an unpainted wooden shed, and a stone building that served as a store. On the opposite side there were a couple of rustic cabins and a few trees. Nobody seemed to be stirring, which pleased Gideon. He didn't want spectators while he searched for the stump of the right tree.

He twisted in the saddle to check his back trail. *Good!* he

★ ★

told himself with satisfaction. *I was right—neither that stranger nor Odell expected me to go looking for the gold this early*.

Gideon rode on to the depot, which was his first landmark. Across from it, he turned the mule to the right, heading for the approximate place where he had been knocked out when thrown from the wagon.

He ground-hitched Hercules at about where he had returned to consciousness. Dismounting, in dismay he surveyed the stumps where a fine stand of trees had stood on July 21. It covered a much larger area than he remembered.

Which one? he asked himself, feeling the enormity of the task before him. He stood for a full minute, hoping Isham wouldn't be angry about his going alone to search for Papa's gold.

Gideon had not wanted to wait for Isham to ask the doctor if it was all right to go into Centreville. No matter what the surgeon said, if anything happened to make Isham worse, Gideon would have felt responsible.

He had awakened to the sound of a rooster crowing and opened his eyes in the Adamses' barn. Feeling it would be safer to search for the gold in daylight, Gideon had quietly risen from the hay, leaving Zeb asleep, then saddled the mule and slipped away without breakfast.

Riding toward Centreville, he recalled his mother saying she hoped that he found the black man who had helped him and his father when they were here before.

The farm wagon had tipped over, their mules had been killed, and Gideon had been knocked unconscious. While he was out, the battle at nearby Bull Run Creek had started, and his father had hurriedly buried the gold they had received for their wheat.

Gideon recalled returning to consciousness to find a big black face with a scraggly beard and deep brown eyes bending

★ ★

over him. The man had grinned at him and grunted, and Gideon's father had joined him.

Later, Mr. Tugwell told his son that the nameless black man had come from nowhere to help the injured boy. When the whipped Yankee invaders streamed by, fleeing from their Confederate defeat at Bull Run Creek, the Negro had brought two Federal horses with blood on their saddles.

Still without a word, he had helped father and son mount, then slapped the horses into a run. The last they saw of him as they galloped toward safety in the Shenandoah Valley, he was standing watching them.

Gideon shook off the memories and tried to think which one of the tree stumps marked the site where the gold was buried. He had forgotten about Oakley Odell until he heard a heavy footstep behind him. He whirled around in fear.

★ ★

A RIBBON FOR
HER HAIR

Gideon brought his hands up in an instinctive protective motion, expecting to be attacked by Odell. Instead, he faced a big black man wearing rough slave clothing. He had a scraggly beard, deep brown eyes, and white teeth that flashed in a friendly smile.

"Oh!" Gideon exclaimed, lowering his hands and smiling in relief. "You scared me!"

The slave dropped his eyes contritely but didn't speak. Gideon recalled that he had not spoken when he had helped Gideon and his father escape to their home after the Union defeat.

"I remember you!" Gideon cried. "You're the one who helped my father after I was knocked unconscious when our wagon tipped over the day of the Battle at Bull Run Creek."

The black man raised his eyes and silently nodded. Gideon rushed on. "Later, you brought a couple of Yankee horses whose owners had been killed in that battle. Thanks to you, Papa and I escaped through the Shenandoah Valley."

A slight shrug of his shoulders indicated that the slave felt he hadn't done anything special.

Gideon explained. "I'm glad to see you because we didn't really get a chance to thank you back then." Impulsively, he stuck out his hand.

The black man drew back in surprise.

★ ★

Gideon was surprised, too. *What am I doing? A white boy shaking hands with a slave!*

"You saved our lives," Gideon said quickly, leaving his hand extended. "I don't have anything to give you, but I am very grateful."

The white teeth flashed again, and the big, work-hardened hand closed briefly over the boy's. "No white 'un ever give me nothin' like dis! I'se Linus. Massa let me work out fo' hire."

The slave dialect was a little hard for Gideon to understand, but he realized that this man's owner trusted him not to run away and hired him out to whoever would pay for his services. Gideon knew that a slave in such an arrangement did not receive anything. All he earned went to the master.

"My name's Gideon," the boy said. "You're Linus?"

Nodding, the slave asked, "Y'all come fo' de buryin'?" He motioned toward the tree stumps. "I'se 'spected y'all to be back fo' dat."

Gideon's heart seemed to skip a beat at the realization that Linus had apparently seen Mr. Tugwell bury the gold. A fearful thought made Gideon tense. *I hope he didn't dig it up!*

Gideon tried to keep his voice from revealing that fear. "The trees are all cut down, but do you know where Papa buried . . . uh . . . it?"

Linus nodded but didn't speak.

Breathlessly, Gideon asked, "Is it still there?"

Nodding again, Linus started to lift an arm toward the stumps where the trees had stood, but Gideon reached out suddenly and stopped the motion.

"Please don't point!"

The brown eyes opened wide, so Gideon glanced around and hastily explained. "Someone has been following me. I need to get that . . . uh . . . buried stuff dug up, but I don't want anyone to see me."

With another quick look around, Gideon continued. "Linus, please walk me out near where you saw my father bury

★ ★

something, but don't go directly to that stump. Walk off to one side and then stop directly across from it, then use your eyes to motion to the right tree. Just don't go near it in case we're being watched. Will you do that?"

"Sho' 'nuf." The grin flashed again as though Linus were enjoying a game. He started off toward the tree stumps, his poorly fitting shoes sliding up and down on his heels.

Gideon followed, looking in all directions, but there were only a couple of men walking together down the rutted street. They didn't look toward Gideon and Linus. There was no sign of Odell.

Gideon turned around just as Linus stopped and stared toward some stumps twenty feet away. The farm boy's keen eyes quickly discerned a stump with smooth bark. Nearby was a single long cone that he was sure didn't have any prickles.

He confirmed it was from a white pine by spotting a dried clump of needles resting partly upright against the stump. He was sure that when he could get closer he would find that the needles grew in groups of five.

"I see it," Gideon said softly. "I'm going to get a shovel. Thanks for your help."

Linus grinned. "I'se go wo'k now," he replied and walked away.

Gideon watched him go, silently praying that the gold was still under that nearby white pine stump. When Linus rounded a corner and was lost to sight, Gideon retrieved the shovel from where he had secured it to the mule's saddle. After again looking carefully to make sure that Odell or nobody else was paying any attention to him, Gideon returned to the stump that Linus had indicated.

Kicking small sticks and other debris aside, Gideon stuck the shovel point into the earth. It slid down easily, indicating that the soil had recently been disturbed. With rapidly beating heart, Gideon dug quickly until he heard a metallic clink.

That's it! He wanted to shout with relief, but he contained

★ ★

himself. Using his hands, he removed the last of the dirt. He recognized his father's old homemade handkerchief with one corner torn off. It was dirty but wrapped around something.

Bending low over the hole so that nobody could see, Gideon rapidly unwrapped the cloth. "Thank the Lord!" he exclaimed aloud at the sight of the gold coins. A quick count confirmed that there were thirteen twenty-dollar gold pieces worth $260. Gideon wanted to shout, *It's all here! More than some men at home earn in a whole year!*

With another quick look around, Gideon slid the wrapped coins inside his shirt, kicked dirt back into the hole, grabbed the shovel, and returned to the mule.

Very alert, but with forced casualness, he forced himself to ride slowly out of town to avoid arousing any suspicion. He began whistling cheerfully, but his mind warned, *You're not safely home yet, so watch out!*

★　★　★　★　★

Alone in his young master's bedchamber, Nat finished laying out on the bed all the clothes William had ordered prepared for the dance. Nat eyed the dark, form-fitting jacket and matching vest. His fingers lingered on the soft gray pants. Impulsively, Nat wanted to know how he would look in a rich young man's dress clothes.

After glancing at the closed door and listening to make sure nobody was coming down the hall, Nat held the tailored jacket against his chest.

Nice! he told himself approvingly. *If I wore this and William would let me wear a hat over my curly black hair, I could pass as the white son of some wealthy plantation owner.*

"No!" Nat whispered aloud in reproof. "Even though my father was white, the race law says that a child must follow the condition of the slave mother. So I will always be considered as black. Yet I won't always be a slave! Neither will my mother, my sister, and three younger brothers. When I get free, I'm going to come back and find—"

"What're you mumbling about?"

William's voice from the doorway jerked Nat around as though he were on strings. Hastily, he lowered the jacket and headed back to lay it on the bed with the rest of the clothing.

House slaves were not allowed to speak until asked a question or required to say something. Nat was so startled that his mouth suddenly dried up in fear, so he didn't reply.

"I can see for myself!" William snapped, rapidly striding across the room. "You were putting on airs! Trying to think of yourself as the equal of a white man!" He slapped Nat sharply across the cheek.

Nat knew better, but he momentarily lost control. Anger erupting inside showed in the fury of his eyes and sudden clenching of teeth.

"Don't you look at me like that, you black imp!" William backhanded Nat hard before he could turn away.

With intense willpower Nat forced the rage from his eyes and relaxed his jaw. He dropped his eyes in a gesture of submission. But inside, the indignity of being slapped outraged him. His stomach twisted into knots, and hot blood scalded through his body.

"You're too uppity!" William continued, his right hand drawn back as though another blow was to be delivered. "I should sell you down the river, or at least send you to the field! Either way, you will learn to respect your superiors!"

Nat forced himself to stand still, his eyes lowered as if accepting the young master's proposed punishment. But there was no submission in Nat's heart. He took refuge in recalling his mother's encouraging final words. *Winning is in the mind and not the muscles.* He comforted himself with the knowledge that in a few days he should be on his way to freedom. He could not risk antagonizing William any further.

"That's better," William said. "You have been obedient up to now. I'll overlook this one stupid error, but you need

★ ★

something to remind you of how close you came to losing all the privileges you enjoy as my personal servant."

Nat flinched at the implied threat but kept his eyes downcast and waited for William's next words.

He said, "You haven't been off the plantation since I bought you. I'm sure you've been looking forward to attending to my needs at the wedding."

Involuntarily, Nat lifted his eyes, anguish filling his mind at what William was suggesting. Escape plans required that Nat first be able to see if his brother Rufus was at the neighboring Darlington Plantation. Instantly, Nat dropped his gaze, but it was too late.

"So!" William cried triumphantly. "It's that important to you, is it? Well, Nat, you just lost that opportunity! I'm going to the wedding, but you're not! You are not to leave Briarstone! Is that understood?"

Nat was so stunned and disappointed that he could only nod briefly.

William turned and strode out of the room, his satisfied laugh indicating he was pleased with himself.

Nat stood in dismayed silence. His plans to check on Rufus had vanished like a puff of smoke in the wind.

★   ★   ★   ★   ★

Emily's excitement rose as she and Julie began choosing accessories for their gowns to be worn to Theodore and Annabelle's wedding. Toby had brought a box of velvet ribbons in and spread them on her young mistress's bed.

Emily was uncomfortable with having a maid given to her, so she had tactfully suggested that Lizzie go search in a hall closet for other possible accessories suitable for a wedding guest.

For a fleeting moment Emily's mind drifted. She remembered some time back when she and Gideon had briefly discussed slavery. Although his father had never owned any,

★ ★

Gideon had told her that slavery seemed natural to him.

Does he still think that? she wondered. She wished she could ask him, but he certainly wouldn't be invited to the wedding.

A slight frown wrinkled her brow as she also recalled their last brief conversation in the river bottom. He had said he was going to visit his brother who had been wounded at Manassas. Then he had abruptly ridden off, saying someone was following him.

Who was following him, and why? Oh, I hope nothing's happened to him and he gets back before I leave for Illinois.

Julie's voice intruded into Emily's reverie.

"How about this one?" Julie asked.

"What?" Emily asked, trying to refocus her thoughts.

"I said, what about this one?" Julie held a scarlet velvet ribbon against her hair for Emily's evaluation.

"Very nice. It's just the right contrast for your dark hair. Maybe you should secure it with something in the middle above your forehead."

"Good idea." Julie picked up a tiny white bird and held it in place, then checked her image in the mirror.

"I like it," she decided and turned to her maid. "Toby, fix this when you finish with my gown. Now, Emily, how about this ribbon for your hair? It will show off your blond curls real well."

Before Emily could reply, Aunt Anna opened the bedchamber door and entered without invitation. "Are you two girls ever going to finish primping?" she asked with a hint of disapproval in her tone.

"We're almost done," Julie answered. "What do you think of this to go with my green silk dress, Mama?"

She replied without interest, "It doesn't matter what you two wear because everyone's eyes will be on the bride. So let this go and come down to supper."

Aunt Anna started out the door, then paused to add, "Wil-

liam just came downstairs all upset because he found Nat trying on his good clothes and so has forbidden him to leave this
plantation instead of going to the wedding with us."

"Oh, I'm sorry!" Emily exclaimed, causing both her aunt
and cousin to look at her in surprise. Emily floundered, unable
to think why she had blurted out such a thing about a slave.

She explained lamely, "I know how much I'm looking forward to going, so it must be much more so for a slave who
never gets to leave—"

"Servant!" Aunt Anna broke in angrily. "We do not call
them 'slaves.'"

"I forgot," Emily replied. "I'm sorry."

Aunt Anna shook her head in disapproval. "You seem determined to never learn to accept our way of life."

She left the room, adding from outside the hallway door,
"Now, girls, please come downstairs."

When her mother's footsteps receded down the hallway,
Julie said softly, "Emily, you've got to be more careful what you
say around Mama and my brother."

"I know, but sometimes it just slips out."

"You're going to do that once too often, then they probably
will be glad to see you leave."

Emily didn't reply but thought, *It's a terrible thing to do,
but that's what I'm counting on. It's the only way I know how
to get permission to go back home.*

A THIEF IN THE NIGHT

Isham looked upset as he waited on the front porch of the farmhouse when Gideon rode up and dismounted.

Isham hastily lifted his wounded arm with the other and arose to stomp across the wooden porch toward his younger brother. "You went off alone again! I should box your ears for sure this time!"

Gideon grinned. "You won't when you see what I've got." He patted his shirt. "Right here. All of it!"

Isham let out a happy cry as Gideon led the mule toward the steps. He dropped his voice to quickly relate his morning's experiences.

When he had finished, Isham clapped him on the back. "You got a reason to be proud, little brother!"

He grinned. "Maybe Papa was wrong and I can do something right."

"Don't hold that against him, Gideon. He doesn't know how much words can hurt. He doesn't understand that I always loved farm work but you don't. It's hard to do something well when you don't like it."

"I can hardly wait to get home and hand him this." Gideon again touched the lump inside his shirt. "Of course," he added quickly, "we aren't there yet, so we've got to watch out for Odell."

"We'll have to fool him somehow."

★ ★

"We?"

"I'm hoping the surgeon will give me a medical furlough for a few days. Now, let's figure out the safest place to keep the money until we can head home."

A boyish shout from the road drew both brothers' attention. Zeb waved vigorously from where he sat in the single seat of a buggy driven by Carolyn.

"He sounds happy," Gideon observed.

The brothers walked down the steps to the fence as Carolyn called "Whoa" to the horse.

Zeb leaped from the stopped vehicle without touching the step. His clothes were washed, his face was clean, and his hair was combed. Grinning, he ran to meet the brothers at the fence.

"Guess what? I'm a-gonna be a drummer boy!"

Gideon returned the grin, but his insides lurched at the boyish enthusiasm. Gideon was aware of how much Zeb reminded him of his little brother, Ben. It hurt to even think of Ben facing the dangers of war. Even though Gideon had only known Zeb a short time, he was still only a little ten-year-old boy going unarmed into battle, taking the same risks as grown-up soldiers.

Isham stuck his left hand across the fence and gripped Zeb's right hand. "Congratulations!"

Zeb stood straight, sucked in his stomach, and threw out what little chest he had. "Oh, it wasn't easy, mind you! At first that ol' cap'n turned me down because I didn't know how to play a drum."

He paused dramatically before rushing on, his voice high with excitement. "But I done looked him right smack dab in the eye an' said, 'I bet none of them so'jers knowed how to march an' shoot straight when they come to this here camp, but you didn't send them packin', did you?'"

The boy turned to the young woman as she and Isham smiled at each other. "Ain't that jist what I said?"

★ ★

"It certainly is." Carolyn gave him a warm smile, but Gideon noticed that her eyes seemed sad. Could she be having the same kind of scary thoughts as Gideon?

She urged Zeb, "Tell them what else you said."

"Well," the boy continued, fairly bursting with satisfaction, "I done told him one of the boys from another company could teach me the drum calls. That cap'n, he allowed as how that was possible, and seein' as how his Company B's drummer boy was down with fever, I could take his place. So I got in!"

Gideon noticed that Isham's eyes had shifted to Carolyn. She seemed not to notice, but Gideon saw a pink blush on her cheeks.

"Zeb can be very persuasive," Carolyn said.

"I report tomorrow," Zeb said proudly. "Gideon, I reckon y'all will jist have to go home without me."

Gideon nodded glumly but didn't speak, knowing what dangers Zeb faced in a soldier's world.

Carolyn said, "Maybe you won't have to go home alone, Gideon." She switched her gaze from him to Isham. "Don't get your hopes up just yet, but I talked to the surgeon. He's a friend of my father's, so I took the liberty of mentioning you. The doctor will be here this afternoon to take another look at your arm."

Isham's eyes suddenly lit up. "Are you saying that he's considering letting me go home to recuperate?"

"I'm just relaying what he told me," she protested. "I don't know what his decision will be."

Gideon's voice reflected his excitement. "But there's a chance, isn't there, Miss Carolyn?"

"I hope so, for both your sakes. I'll put the horse up and then we can all talk some more."

"I'll help you," Isham volunteered.

As the pair walked away, Zeb turned serious eyes on Gideon. "You don't look none too happy for me."

"If that's what you want, I'm glad for you." Gideon didn't

★ ★

103

want to voice his concerns. "Tell me what your duties will be as a drummer boy."

Zeb needed no encouragement, cheerfully rattling off responsibilities that sent a shiver through Gideon. "When I ain't beatin' out commands to the so'jers on my drum, I get to be a barber, tote water, sharpen the doctors' operatin' tools, carry stretchers, be what they call a med'cal 'sistant, an' he'p cook. They ain't no big kitchen in our army. A few so'jers git together as messmates an' do their own cookin' and sech like."

"Sounds like you'll be busy," Gideon said absently, his thoughts drifting. *I sure hope Isham can go home with me in case Odell tries to take the gold. I also hope that Papa's all right and that Emily hasn't left for Illinois yet.* Gideon sighed. *Maybe I'd better do some praying about this.*

★　★　★　★　★

William sent Nat to the barn to saddle his favorite horse so he could ride around the plantation on an inspection tour with the overseer. Nat took the saddled animal by the halter and led him in front of the carriage house, where George sat outside smoking his pipe. Nat stopped the horse and pretended to tighten the saddle girth.

He spoke softly without looking at the old coachman. "Tell me more about this boy at Darlington that you said looks like me."

"I told you all I know. He's about twelve and looks enough like you to be your brother."

"Have you talked to him?"

"No reason. I just saw him. But while all the white folks are at the wedding, maybe I could find him and ask some questions for you."

Nat wasn't surprised that news of his being confined to Briarstone had already reached George. "Thanks, but that wouldn't do much good. Even if it is Rufus, I would have to talk to him myself."

★　★

"That could be mighty dangerous." George's tone carried a hint of alarm. "If you get caught going or coming, you might not ever again get a chance to cross over Jordan."

"I know." Nat straightened up and reached for the horse's halter. "But I've got to be sure."

"If it is Rufus, you got another problem. There's only room for two to cross. What then?"

"I'll decide after I know about my brother." Nat led the horse toward the big house as fear battled with hope over the risk he must take the following night.

★ ★ ★ ★ ★

The surgeon arrived mid-morning, checked all the patients, and finished with Isham. "Take care of that arm," he said, closing his little black bag, "and you can go home for ten days."

Gideon started to shout with joy, but Isham asked the doctor, "Starting when?"

"Carolyn has already spoken to the major. He told me that if I think you're fit, he'll have the necessary papers signed and delivered here by orderly yet today."

This led to hurried preparations with Carolyn, her father and Zeb helping. Isham was unable to handle a musket because of his wounded right arm, so Mr. Adams loaned him a loaded Remington .44 caliber army six-shooter, and a mule called Caesar. Both were to be returned when Isham reported back to Camp Pickens at the end of his furlough.

When Isham and Carolyn went to the barn to get the mule, Zeb sidled up to Gideon. "You know what, Gideon? I think she likes me."

"Carolyn?" he asked absently.

Nodding, Zeb explained. "Before she would take me to see that cap'n, she washed my clothes and made me take a bath."

Puzzled, Gideon asked, "Why does that make you think she likes you?"

"Well, after my ma and pa died, an' before I run away from my uncle, nobody ever cared much what I did. But Miss Carolyn said flat out that if'n I didn't take a bath, she wouldn't innerduce me to that cap'n friend of hers."

"I see," Gideon replied, amused. "Other people do care about you, Zeb."

"Really?"

Gideon studied the earnest face. "I'm sure of it, and I'm going to pray for you, same as I do for Ben."

Zeb blinked as though in surprise. "Ain't nobody prayed fer me since my ma died."

When he left, Gideon stepped to the window at the sound of a galloping horse coming. A uniformed rider reined in his mount and handed some papers to Isham. He tore them open, skimmed them, then turned to Carolyn standing by him. Gideon couldn't hear what was said, but his brother's big smile told him what he needed to know.

"Thank God, we're going home!"

★　★　★　★　★

While Julie practiced the piano, Emily wandered down to the river bottom where she and Gideon had met before. She told herself that she was just going for a walk, but she knew that wasn't entirely true.

She heard the ring of an ax and headed toward the sound. Soon the Tugwells' two hounds caught her scent and ran toward her through the underbrush. Their deep baying frightened her. She cried out, "Gideon! It's Emily! Call off your dogs."

Instantly, there was a sharp whistle, which slowed the hounds but did not stop them. They ceased baying but quartered toward her, long ears flopping loudly.

"It's all right," she greeted the dogs as they circled around in back of her. She turned with them, not quite sure she trusted them.

★　★

"Rock! Red!" the voice commanded firmly from behind her. "Down! Down, I say!"

As they obeyed, Emily was surprised to see Gideon's younger brother. "Ben!" she exclaimed, "I thought you were Gideon." It was the first time Emily had talked to Ben since the last day at school that spring.

"He's not back yet." The ten-year-old approached shyly, uncombed hair tumbling over his eyes.

"Oh," Emily replied, disappointed. "Shouldn't he have been home by now?"

"No, not yet, but our folks are getting somewhat concerned. Papa is mad at himself for letting Gideon go off all alone to get the . . . uh . . . to see if he could find out anything about our older brother. He got wounded near Manassas."

"Yes, Gideon told me before he left. I hope he's safely home soon."

"Thanks. After he left we did get a letter from Isham. Well, sort of. He didn't write it. He had some woman do that because he was wounded in his right arm."

"Oh, I'm sorry! Is he recovering well?"

"He wrote that he's getting better, but he'll have to stay in this family's home with some other wounded men for a while. Papa says Isham didn't want us to worry, but it's hard not knowing for sure if he is really going to be all right."

"I would expect him to be in a hospital."

"Me too, but Papa says there probably wasn't enough of them for all the wounded. The letter said this family took in Isham and some others that were hurt."

"I see." Emily gazed thoughtfully across the river. "Gideon's probably all right and staying with his brother until he gets back."

"That's what Mama says, but Papa sees it different. He's afraid something happened to Gideon."

Emily caught her breath. "Like what?"

"Well, there are all kinds of dangers on the road with Yankees running loose, plus ornery people of all kinds. Sometimes Papa gets real mad at himself for letting Gideon go off alone. It's his first time ever, so Papa says he'll go down to his grave knowing it was his fault if anything terrible did happen to Gideon. Mama says God will take care of him and that Papa is only blaming himself because he's so sick."

"What's wrong?"

"Doctor said it's his heart," Ben replied soberly. "Papa's so worried that he's talking about going to look for Gideon, but Mama says he's not well enough to do that. She says all we can do is pray and wait."

Emily's head nodded in agreement. "I'll join your family in doing that. Well, I have to get back." She started to turn away, then again looked at Ben.

"I expect to be leaving here in a few days, so if I'm gone when Gideon returns, would you tell him—?"

"Where're you going?" Ben interrupted.

"Back to Illinois, I hope. So if I don't see Gideon, would you tell him that I said to never give up his dream?"

"His dream?"

"About becoming a writer."

"Oh, that. Papa says that's foolishness. He says it's like Gideon always going off chasing butterflies instead of plowing or working on our land."

"I respect your father, Ben, but I don't think it's foolishness for Gideon, or anyone else, to reach for the stars in whatever way he wants. So would you tell Gideon to keep dreaming and reaching?"

"Yes, but I hope he gets home before you leave."

"So do I, Ben," she said softly, turning back toward Briarstone. *But unless he gets here in the next few days, I may never know if he's alive or dead. In fact, I may never see him again—certainly not until the war is over.*

She began running toward the plantation just before a broken sob escaped her lips.

★ ★

★ ★ ★ ★ ★

Within an hour of Isham receiving his orders, he and Gideon had said hasty good-byes and rode their mules over to the Warrenton Turnpike. It wasn't the fastest way home, but it offered the best opportunity to watch their back trail. They thought that Odell would not be expecting Gideon to be with a uniformed Confederate soldier armed with a Union revolver.

It was dusk when the brothers were stopped by two pickets. As they examined Isham's papers, he said, "My little brother here said he didn't see a single picket when he rode up yesterday. So how come you're on guard duty here tonight?"

The soldier returned Isham's papers, saying, "Our cavalrymen have been chasing some mounted Yankees. You best keep an eye out. If they see your uniform, they might draw down on you. You won't have much chance against them with only one weapon between you."

"We'll get by," Isham said, then asked, "Have you seen any civilian riding this way?"

When both pickets shook their heads, the brothers rode on. "Gid," Isham said with satisfaction, "I think we fooled Odell. So let's find a stream and make camp." They left the road and camped in a grove of trees by a creek. The brothers took turns sleeping with the saddlebags of gold next to them under their blankets. The other brother stood guard with the revolver. Gideon was familiar with muskets, but Isham had to show him how to handle the pistol.

The stars were starting to fade, and the fire had burned low when Gideon neared the end of his watch. It was so peaceful and still under the trees that he had to struggle to stay awake.

I'd better go splash water on my face so I don't fall asleep, he told himself. He looked around and assured himself that no one was around. He went down to the creek and washed his face with cold water. Feeling better, he started back toward camp. The fire flared up, showing a shadowy figure straightening up from where he had been bending over the sleeping Isham.

"Look out, Isham!" Gideon shouted, bringing up the unfamiliar pistol.

The figure half spun toward Gideon, then leaped over Isham, who sleepily raised up in his blankets.

Gideon started to aim the gun but didn't fire for fear of hitting his brother. As the figure disappeared into the dense trees, Gideon sprinted wildly toward the campfire, where Isham tried to scramble to his feet. He cried out in pain from using his wounded arm.

In panic Gideon cried, "Are you all right?"

"Yes." Isham was half asleep. "What's going on?"

Gideon reached his brother. "Somebody was bending over you." Gideon threw back Isham's cover and moaned in despair. "The gold is gone!"

★ ★

A PRISONER OF WAR

When daylight came, Gideon was almost literally sick with a guilty conscience for letting Odell steal the saddlebags of gold coins. In the dusty road he and Isham found where Odell's horse had been tied while the theft was made. The tracks led toward Church Creek.

Gideon cried hopefully. "Maybe we can catch him!"

"Our mules can't match his horse's pace. Before we can get there, he will have met Barley Cobb and turned over our money to him."

"Then we'll go after Cobb and get it back!"

"Hold on! There's no proof that he's involved, and he would deny it if we accused him."

"But we've got to do something! I can't face Papa without that money because it was my fault I let Odell sneak up on our camp like that."

"But I was wrong in thinking we had fooled him."

"Don't blame yourself. I got careless. Oh, Isham! What will this do to Papa? Now he can't have the medicine he needs. So maybe he was right when he said I can't do anything right."

"Stop beating up on yourself and try to think of ways to outsmart Odell."

Gideon snatched at any hope of redeeming himself. He suggested, "How about leaving the road and cutting across the fields? Maybe we can get ahead of him."

★ ★

"It's worth a try, little brother."

Soon the brothers were mounted and cutting across country, pushing the mules hard in the morning sun, but Gideon could not shake the terrible guilt he felt.

By mid-morning he couldn't stand it any longer. Riding side by side with Isham, Gideon said, "If this doesn't work and Papa dies . . ."

"Don't start that again!"

"Please, Isham! I'm trying to face facts. If we don't get that gold back and lose Papa, then it's a sure bet that William Lodge will try to force Mama and the rest of us off the farm."

"I think he would try that."

"He and his father have wanted to get our place for a long time. In ten days you have to report back to the army. That leaves me as the oldest at home, so I'll have to find a way to keep the farm. It's the only way we can make a living, such as it is."

"Papa would turn over in his grave if William and his father got our farm. But as much as you hate farming, and with only Ben to help, I don't see how you could hang on to the place."

"Neither do I, but my conscience wouldn't let me lose out to William."

"We'll deal with that when and if we have to. Now, tell me more about your new Yankee friend."

A picture of Emily flickered through Gideon's mind. He fervently hoped that she had not left for Illinois. Then he felt guilty for thinking of his own selfish wants and forced thoughts of Emily away.

"I'd rather hear what it was like when you fought the Yankees at Manassas," he said. "Were you scared of dying after you got shot?"

"I'm not sure *scared* is the right word, but I thought I was. Lying there all alone, seeing my blood soaking into the ground when I couldn't stop it. I prayed like I never have in my life. But the hours passed, and I could feel myself getting weaker."

★ ★

Gideon visualized the scene with dead Union and Confederates all around, while Isham's life ebbed out of a musket ball wound.

"What did you think about?" he asked softly.

"Lots of things, but the strangest happened just before they found me. I thought I heard bugles calling, and I tried to go to them but couldn't."

"Bugles from Camp Pickens?"

"No, they weren't like any I've heard before. These were sort of in my head, yet seemed real. It's hard to explain, but, well, I had to go where they called—even to death."

After a thoughtful silence, Gideon said, "It's not the same, yet somehow that's sort of what I hear in my head: a call to write, no matter what."

"The time will come when you can answer that call, little brother. Just be patient."

"I know; first things first."

The brothers rode on in companionable silence until the sun started down the western sky. They entered a line of trees where Isham suddenly jerked back on Caesar's reins. "Whoa!" he commanded sharply.

Gideon yanked Hercules to a halt. "What is it?"

"See them?" Isham asked softly. "Cavalrymen coming this way. But are they ours or Federals?"

"They must be ours. The Yankees all ran back to Washington after Manassas."

"Their infantrymen did, but you can be sure that the Union commanders have mounted troops left behind to scout around. Cavalrymen are the only eyes and ears the generals have to find out where their enemy is."

Gideon glanced at his brother's tattered gray Confederate infantryman uniform. "If they're Yankees and they see you . . ."

"I know. They'll want me for a prisoner. Let's get down and out of sight until—"

He broke off as one of the horsemen shouted from where

he had suddenly stood up in the saddle. His blue uniform was clearly visible.

"They're Yankees!" Isham exclaimed. "Run for it!"

Gideon imitated his older brother, leaning forward along Hercules' neck so that the coarse mane stung his face while his heels beat a frantic tattoo against the mule's flanks. A quick look back under his armpit showed that the Union cavalrymen were gaining rapidly.

Isham yelled over the sound of pounding hooves, "It's no use! They don't want you, so I'll turn off and let them follow me. You get home to Papa!"

"No! I don't want to leave you."

"Don't argue! They must be looking for prisoners in hopes of getting Confederate information. This is the only way! Ready? Now!"

Isham turned sharply away. Gideon reluctantly kept Hercules running straight ahead. The Federals shouted in triumph and thundered after Isham. An anguished cry tore Gideon's throat when he vanished behind a line of trees with the troopers almost upon him.

Gideon reined in Hercules and sat staring helplessly toward where his brother was now surely a Yankee prisoner. A hot mist seared Gideon's eyes as he slowly turned the mule's head toward home. He had lost the gold, and now his brother was a Yankee prisoner. Gideon shuddered at what this news would do to Papa.

★ ★ ★ ★ ★

In the few months that Nat had been in the big house at Briarstone, he had often heard the music and merriment from the barn but had never been able to attend the Saturday night slave events. His duties as a personal body servant to William required Nat to be close by to render any service desired.

Tonight, William had confined Nat to Briarstone, so he could have attended the dance. Instead, Nat braced himself for the dangerous trip to Darlington in hopes of finding his brother Rufus. If he was there, they could escape together.

After William and his mother, sister, and cousin Emily drove away in the big coach with George at the reins, Nat walked outside under the light of a nearly full moon. He looked across the broad-leafed tobacco plants to where lights faintly showed at Darlington Plantation.

"Are you going to the dance?" a soft voice asked from behind Nat.

He turned to see Sarah. She had replaced her usual shapeless slave shift with a calico dress that made Nat's eyes open wide in surprise. "Uh, maybe later."

"Look," she said, extending her ankle from under the long dress. "No shackle. Hattie, the cook, she got it taken off. She told the mistress that it got in the way while I'm helping in the kitchen. No slave has more power with white folks than a good cook."

After Sarah walked on toward the barn, Nat looked around carefully to make sure nobody was watching. Then he slipped across the grounds toward Darlington.

★ ★ ★ ★ ★

It was Emily's first visit to Darlington, and she was impressed. The manor house was one long, single-story frame building painted white with green trim. Two of the new Confederate flags graced the white pillars flanking the main entrance. The blue union, containing a circle of seven white stars, with one broad white stripe and two red ones seemed strange to her.

A handsome, light-skinned slave in a formal black suit flashed a welcoming smile and held the heavy front door open for Emily, her aunt, and both cousins.

Just inside the spacious entryway with its huge crystal chandelier of coal-oil lamps, Emily curtsied when introduced to the groom's parents, Mr. and Mrs. Theodore Cummings, Sr.;

★ ★

and Mr. and Mrs. Frank Harper, the bride's parents.

Emily was dazzled at how grand they looked, as did the well-dressed guests making their way through a door to the right. Emily was conscious that everyone kept stealing glances at her. She knew it wasn't just to admire her blue taffeta dress with the lace ruffles, or even her golden hair, which reflected the lamplight.

From behind a flared fan that matched her green dress, Julie almost giggled. "You're getting more notice than the bride will. Come on. I'll introduce you to the people our age, but don't be hurt if some of them act a little cool toward you."

Emily managed an understanding smile. "I don't blame them for being careful around such a dangerous person as a twelve-year-old Yankee girl. How do they know I'm not really the spy some people think I am?"

"I'm glad you can joke about it. Let's start with these friends over here."

The girls entered a long, narrow room that Julie said had been especially made for dancing. Chairs had been set up on both sides of an aisle that led to the temporary altar where the wedding would be performed. Later, all furniture would be removed so that dancers would have a totally obstacle-free hardwood floor. Emily followed Julie through the crowds of guests streaming through the door and being ushered to seats. It was a far more grand scene than Emily had ever seen in her middle-class Illinois community.

She frowned, thinking that all this luxurious living was made possible for the host planter family by slaves who met their every need.

Watch what you're thinking! Emily warned herself while her eyes enjoyed the room, which had been decorated with red and yellow roses and smaller hand-sewn replicas of the Confederate flag. The result was a combination of more traditional wedding purity and a tribute to the soldier-groom and the new nation guests now claimed as theirs.

★ ★

Making their way through a cluster of men still standing and talking, Emily caught snatches of conversation about the war. In a few steps she heard that it was generally quiet in Virginia, but there had been some military action in the western part of the state and elsewhere in the South.

She caught another comment from a gray-haired man with a cane who asked his companion, "Did you hear about our bishop at Manassas?"

Julie nudged Emily and whispered, "He means Bishop Porter of our church. He's also an artillery captain."

Emily didn't reply but concentrated on catching the older man's words.

"When our gallant troops from the Thirty-Third Virginia in their blue uniforms overran Federal gunners at that battle—"

A male listener interrupted. "Was that where our boys were mistaken by the Yankees until too late?"

"The same. As you know, not all of our troops have gray uniforms. So the Federals hesitated in firing at our approaching boys, who cut them down and seized their cannon."

Taking a quick breath, the speaker concluded, "When Bishop Porter saw that from where his cannon had run out of ammunition, he and some of his artillerymen rushed over and turned the Yankees' guns on them. They ran, but every time the captured cannon was loaded, Bishop Porter called out, 'May God have mercy on their souls—fire!' "

Emily involuntarily gasped. Suddenly, the war seemed very real and close to home. She hurried after Julie, who was still making her way toward some young people clustered together for peer comfort in this environment of adults.

A hand closed on Emily's wrist, making her stop in surprise. She looked into the deep blue eyes of a short, elderly woman wearing wire-rimmed spectacles. Beautiful silver hair, parted in the middle, crowned a wrinkle-free face ending in a determined-looking square chin.

"Pardon me," she said, smiling pleasantly. "You must be Emily Lodge."

Emily nodded, glancing at Julie, who said, "Yes, she is. Emily, this is Mrs. Clara Yates. That's her husband over there with those men."

Mrs. Yates said, "Emily, I would like to chat with you sometime this evening."

Julie hurriedly excused herself and walked away.

Emily glanced around to see if William was watching but didn't see him.

"I can help you with your plans to get home to Illinois," Mrs. Yates added, still smiling.

Emily stared, surprised that anyone outside of Briarstone could have heard about that. Then she remembered that white families indiscreetly spoke in front of slaves, and the Yateses had freedmen working for them. There was surely a slave-and-freedman grapevine, which meant Mrs. Yates had a direct connection not only inside the Lodges' big house, but probably also in other planters' homes.

Emily lowered her voice. "Can you help me find an adult traveling companion to Richmond?"

"Yes, of course. I can also give you a letter of introduction to influential people, including a fine Christian woman there who will give you room and board for a few days. I can also help you obtain a pass to cross Union picket lines into Illinois."

The words were spoken quietly but with calm assurance. "You can do all that?" Emily blurted.

"Yes, indeed. My husband is leaving in a few days for Richmond to deliver some young peach trees he's grown on our farm. He'll have room in the wagon for you and your trunk. So how about meeting me in the garden as soon as possible to discuss details?"

Emily hesitated, hardly able to believe what seemed to be sudden answers to her prayers. Then she glimpsed William

★ ★

hurriedly pushing his way through wedding guests toward her. His face showed disapproval.

To avoid a scene, Emily lowered her voice and told Mrs. Yates, "I'll be there shortly."

Emily breathed a sigh of relief when William slowed his approach and turned away, apparently satisfied at breaking up the conversation.

Emily found Julie and told her she wanted to go outside alone for a few minutes. She walked along a moonlit path between rows of fragrant roses to where Mrs. Yates stood, her eyes looking skyward.

She observed, "The heavens are so beautiful and especially the North Star. Every time I see it, I think of the nearly three million human beings who are slaves in our own land. Many look at that star and wish they could follow it north to freedom. In fact, among the many songs slaves sing with meaning hidden from their masters is one called 'Follow the Drinking Gourd.' That really refers to the North Star."

Emily stirred uneasily, glancing toward the house. "I can't stay long. The wedding will be starting soon."

"I understand," Mrs. Yates said. "Let me be frank for a moment longer, my dear, then I will answer your questions about how to get to your Northern home. If you had an opportunity, would you help one of those slaves find the way to freedom?"

It was a startling question, and warnings went off in Emily's mind. Still, she immediately thought of Nat and decided to take a chance with Mrs. Yates.

"William's and my father were brothers, but Uncle Silas never spoke to Papa again after he began to believe that slavery was wrong. Before my uncle joined the Confederate cavalry, I got in trouble with him because of what I said against slavery. Since then, I've also had some problems with my aunt and William. So it's no secret where I stand on slavery."

"That answers my question. If you can persuade your aunt and William to let you leave, have your trunk packed before

* *

dawn next Monday morning. My husband will pick you up with his wagon at Briarstone."

Emily sucked in her breath at the opportunity. "I'll do my best," she replied with quiet excitement.

"He will see you safely to Richmond and introduce you to an upstanding woman. She will care for you until arrangements are made for your pass into the Union. This may be your only chance—"

She broke off as William charged out of the house toward them.

"Mrs. Yates, please excuse us," he said coldly.

As she nodded and wordlessly walked away, William snapped at Emily, "George will take you home—now!"

"But the wedding . . ."

"Now, I said!"

With no choice Emily turned toward the line of carriages, but she wasn't crushed. Instead, her step was light because her prayers to return to Illinois seemed about to be answered.

★ ★

THE PATROLLER'S
PRISONER

The distant baying of hounds in the river bottom worried Nat until he slipped from the moonlight into the shadowed safety of Darlington's nearest outbuilding. The clean fragrance of wood told him that this was the carpentry shop.

Breathing easier, he cautiously peered around the shop's corner to locate the slave quarters. One of those shacks must be home to the boy Uncle George thought might be Nat's brother. But how could Nat find him, then get back to Briarstone without being caught?

A horse whinnied from the barn and was answered from the line of teams and carriages barely visible in the huge, open yard near the big house. There drivers waited for their masters to need them again.

Nat started to step away from the side of the building when a low voice spoke from the shadows. "I thought you might come here."

Nat turned to run, but the voice stopped him. "Wait! It's me—George."

Still tense, Nat peered closer. In the shadows he not only saw the old reinsman's dark silhouette, but that of a shorter, more slender person. The thought of having anyone else with George made Nat's heart leap again, but instantly he suspected who it might be.

George said, "I saw you coming and brought this young man with me."

"Rufus?" Nat asked eagerly, stepping closer for a better look at the shorter person.

"I'se Johnny," he said in slave dialect. "Don' know nobody name Rufus."

Nat's eyes confirmed that this was not his brother. Nat dropped his head in bitter disappointment.

George said quietly, "I'm sorry. This boy looks so much like you that I hoped . . ."

"It's all right," Nat replied. "Thanks. Now I've got to get back."

He stepped into the moonlight but froze at the sight of two men walking between him and the fence. Their backs were to him, but their clothes indicated they were white. Nat didn't dare be seen by them. Neither could he risk trying to pass the big house and the various carriages and drivers parked around it. That left only one choice.

Bending low and taking advantage of scattered trees and shrubs, he headed toward the river. He was relieved that the dogs' baying was fading away.

★　★　★　★　★

Emily was so startled by William's order for her to go home without getting to see the wedding that she didn't even risk telling Julie. Instead, she hurriedly left Darlington's big house, feeling very conscious of curious eyes upon her. The moon helped her locate the Lodge family's crest marking their best carriage.

The black drivers in their various-colored livery all stopped their small-group conversations as she neared them. She was embarrassed to be the focus of so much curiosity, so she hurried past them and stopped in dismay at the Briarstone carriage. George was not in sight. She turned quickly, eyes probing the night for him. Just as she thought of having to ask one of the other drivers to find him, he hurried toward her.

"There you are!" she exclaimed in relief. "I would like you to take me home now, please."

Emily did not want to embarrass herself by saying anything about what had happened. She told him, "It's all right, George. My cousin William told me to tell you to do this." She wanted to add a face-saving lie, *I'm not feeling well*, but she couldn't.

"Sho' 'nuf," he responded. He quickly reached over and opened the carriage door.

When he had closed it and climbed up to his high outside seat, Emily finally let herself think about what Mrs. Yates had said.

It's everything I've prayed for, Emily reminded herself. *Now all I need is Aunt Anna's and William's permission. I've got to convince them somehow.*

★　★　★　★　★

After leaving Darlington Nat slipped through the river bottom, grateful that the trees blocked most of the moon so he was not easily visible. Disappointment over the boy not being his brother mixed with Nat's anxiety to reach Briarstone without being caught.

The hounds he had heard baying earlier now seemed to be heading his way. Trees in the river bottom cast such dark shadows that Nat could not sight the dogs. He broke into a jog, deciding that they were running about a quarter mile ahead of him. From the direction they were coming, he guessed they could get between him and Briarstone before he got there.

He dodged through the underbrush, unable to avoid crunching dead leaves and small limbs underfoot. They seemed to make unusually loud noises. The hounds might be too far away and making too much noise to hear Nat, but their owner could be closer.

Through the trees to his left, Nat glimpsed the welcome fence line that marked the beginning of the Briarstone property. *Just another few minutes*, he encouraged himself. Increasing his pace, he shot his eyes in all directions, looking for the dogs' owner.

Is he just someone running hounds to train them for this winter's hunts, or is he a patroller?

If he was a hunter, why wasn't he whooping to encourage his dogs? And where was his lantern? It should have been moving, marking the man's progress through the underbrush.

Maybe he's just sitting somewhere. Nat had heard that some poor white men, including patrollers, liked to hear hounds baying on a scent trail as much as treeing a raccoon, opossum, or runaway slave.

Nat kept running in the shelter of the trees, striving for a point just ahead where he could make his cut toward safety. There he would turn left, sprinting from the river bottom across an open area leading to the fence. That was the greatest risk area because he would be fully visible under the moon.

Once over the fence and into Briarstone's tobacco fields, he could go to the barn and be seen there. That would give him an alibi from various witnesses.

I'm going to make it! he thought triumphantly as he neared the next-to-last trees while the hounds were still baying some distance away. *I'm going to—*

His thought snapped like the twigs underfoot at the sight of a kerosene lantern sitting on top of a stump. He stopped instantly, feeling the short hair stand up on his neck. He started to back away into the shadows.

"Hold it! Don't move!"

The white man's harsh voice from behind stabbed through the young slave's body like a knife. He froze as gooseflesh rippled down his shoulders.

"You got a pass, boy?" The question was emphasized by a gun barrel jabbing into Nat's back.

He didn't reply because of sudden terror, knowing he did not, and that his captor was a patroller.

★ ★

"I didn't think so. Which place did you run from?"

When Nat still did not answer, he felt the gun removed from his back. The patroller stepped around in front of his captive, holding a light rifle under his right arm with the barrel aimed at Nat's chest.

"You so much as move a muscle," the patroller warned, "and I'll blow your black heart out!"

With his left hand the man lifted the lantern and held it close to Nat's face. He saw that his captor was unshaven with chewing tobacco stains on his lips.

"I know you, black boy!" he exclaimed with satisfaction. "I done seen you in the village with young William Lodge. You his body servant, huh?"

Nat remained silent, although he overcame some of his fear to boldly look the man in his eyes.

The patroller chuckled. "I knowed it! That's good! Real good! His papa always paid top dollar for runaways, and I reckon young William will, too! Now, you stand right still while I call in my hounds. Then y'all are gonna march right straight up to the big house where I'll git me a big reward!"

★　★　★　★　★

Misery had kept Gideon from getting hungry after sunset, and the early rising of a full moon enabled the mule to pick his way across open farmland toward home. Gideon wasn't anxious to get there, but he knew he had to face his family sooner or later, so he kept riding.

He had felt so good when he and Isham left the Adamses' farm with the gold. Now it was stolen and Isham was a Union prisoner of war.

It will kill Papa when I tell him, and it'll break Mama's heart. It won't be any easier on Ben, Kate, and Lilly, either.

He tried to comfort himself with the knowledge that he couldn't stop the Yankees from seizing Isham. Still, having to report both losses would probably be the hardest thing he had

★　★

ever done. He could not escape the guilty realization that it was his fault that the gold coins had been stolen while he was on picket duty.

His situation seemed so hopeless that Gideon moaned aloud. He muttered, "I should have listened to Papa! I can't do anything right!"

Hercules abruptly shied at something, almost catching Gideon off guard so he had to grab the coarse mane with one hand to keep from being thrown.

"Whoa!" he commanded, pulling back hard on the reins with his other hand and tightening his legs around the mule. "Whoa! Easy now! Easy!"

Hercules settled down, long ears cocked toward the object ahead. Gideon didn't believe mules were skittish like horses, so when he was sure Hercules was calm, he dismounted, keeping a tight grip on the reins.

The object that had spooked the mule fluttered slightly as Gideon approached it. He gingerly touched it with the toe of his shoe, then shook his head. "Hercules, I'm surprised at you. It's nothing but an old cloth." He kicked it, watching it sail through the air in the moonlight. It resembled a handkerchief.

Gideon turned around to remount, then paused. "Hey!" he cried, hastily reaching down and picking up the cloth. He held it so the moonlight struck it fully. "That's Papa's!" He ran his fingers over it, feeling the missing corner and bits of earth that clung to it. "That's the same one he had wrapped around the coins when I dug them up!"

For a moment he stood silently while the full meaning of what he had found impacted him. *Odell fooled Isham and me and also came this way, and now he's ahead of me. But he must not know that, or he wouldn't have thrown the handkerchief away where I might find it.*

Gideon looked into the distance, but even in the light of the full moon there was no sign of the thief.

Springing back into the saddle, Gideon excitedly told the

mule, "Maybe I can get it back!" His voice shot up at that heady thought.

Then reality hit him. *I'm dreaming*, he admitted to himself. *With Isham we might have a chance. But even if I catch up with Odell, what can I do all by myself?*

Self-doubt engulfed Gideon. Should he take the easy way out by avoiding Odell and just going on home? Or should he attempt the seemingly impossible task of somehow recovering his father's gold?

To avoid possibly stumbling upon Odell camped somewhere in the night, Gideon unsaddled the mule, ate cold corn bread, then spread out his blankets.

Staring up at the sky, he realized that tomorrow night he should be home. By then he would either have recovered his father's money, or Odell would have turned it over to Cobb.

The only chance I've got is to somehow outsmart him, he thought. *It would be safer for me if he goes to sleep and I could slip into his camp. All I can do now is wait and hope.*

★　★　★　★　★

Emily changed out of her party dress and waited up until Julie, her aunt, and William returned from the wedding. William only glanced coldly at Emily before going up to his room, but Julie and Aunt Anna invited Emily into the small parlor, where a house servant had built a cheerful blaze in the fireplace.

They didn't say anything about Emily having left before the wedding, confirming her opinion that the subject had been discussed on their carriage ride home. Mother and daughter told Emily in detail about the ceremony, dancing, and visiting afterward.

It was only when their conversations slowed that Emily told them about Mrs. Yates's offer.

Aunt Anna frowned. "I'll tell William in the morning, but he and I have already told you our feelings about your leaving."

★　★

"But Mrs. Yates's offer meets all of his and your conditions for me going," Emily protested. "I think it would be best for all of us to let me accept."

"I'm sorry, Emily," her aunt said, rising. "Now, if you'll excuse me, I'm weary and am going to retire."

When she had gone, Julie pleaded, "Please stop trying to leave! Stay here and do what they want."

"I have bitten my tongue many times, trying to keep quiet about things I think are wrong. I cannot in good conscience never say or do anything about those."

"Yes, you can! My mother never says anything to oppose my father or my brother. Mama had to learn to be subservient, just as I have. So can you."

Emily shook her head. "You were brought up to be that way, and perhaps I would if I had grown up here, but I doubt it because slavery is wrong, and the way they are treated at Briarstone is wrong. I've held my tongue most of the time, but that's not the only reason I want to return to Illinois. It's home, and I want to be there among friends, even if my family is gone. Mrs. Yates has offered me what may be my only chance to start back, so I've got to take it."

Julie said quietly, "You still can't go without permission, and Mr. Yates leaves Monday morning."

"I know there's not much time left, but I believe it's right for me to go. I've prayed that William and Aunt Anna will change their minds. So let's get some sleep and see what tomorrow brings."

★　★　★　★　★

Emily hoped to catch William at breakfast because it was Sunday and he would not have left to supervise activities on the plantation. She was disappointed to see only Aunt Anna and Julie being seated by their personal servants.

As they said good-morning to each other, the maid assigned

to Emily pulled a chair out for her. She said quietly, "Thank you, Lizzie, but I'll do it."

The maid stepped back to stand ready behind her in imitation of the other two servants. "Where's William?" Emily asked.

"You don't want to talk to him this morning," her aunt replied. "Last night a patroller caught one of the servants off the plantation without a pass. William is trying to find out where he went and why, but Nat won't tell. So he's about to be punished."

"Nat?" Emily exclaimed. "His body slave?"

"Servant! Body servant!" Aunt Anna exclaimed.

Julie shot Emily a warning look just as a shrill shriek of pain split the air. Emily leaped up suddenly, almost tipping the chair over on Lizzie. "I can't stand it!" She turned quickly to the door as a second scream penetrated the room.

"Don't go out there!" her aunt warned.

Emily didn't reply but lifted her skirts and ran outside, then through the English box hedges toward the slave quarters. There field hands were gathered in a circle to watch the punishment as a warning.

Nat's hands were secured to the top of a post by leather wristbands. He was stripped to the waist and stretched out so his feet barely touched the ground. Emily was startled to see that William stood by him, feet braced, the whip drawn back to deliver another stroke.

Emily and Julie had first seen Nat on the auction block where William bought him. At that time Julie had explained that a back free of scars indicated that he was not a troublemaker or hadn't tried to escape. Now his bare back glistened with freshly drawn blood.

William dropped the whip and picked up a wooden bucket, making Emily gasp. She had heard about salt water being thrown onto fresh wounds to increase pain. "Stop, William! Oh, please stop!"

★ ★

He angrily spun to face her. "This is none of your concern! He's being punished! Now, get back inside!"

She kept running forward, exclaiming, "That's not punishment! That's torture!"

William turned from her and threw the salt water onto Nat's back, making him screech and writhe in agony. "Leave him there!" he ordered the slaves standing by.

Without another word he grabbed Emily's wrist and started furiously dragging her toward the big house.

★ ★

THE STORM
BREAKS

Emily and William were barely inside the house when he released her arm and started yelling at her.

"What's the matter with you? Don't you know that inter-fering with punishment of a servant is the same as challenging my authority in front of them? That weakens my position in their eyes and could lead to another slave uprising like the one Nat Turner led! We could all be murdered in our beds, and that would be your fault."

Emily had planned to be quiet and take her cousin's verbal abuse, but his statement was unfair.

She exclaimed, "I don't believe that! Those poor people know I was trying to help Nat!"

"Don't argue with me, Emily! I will not keep a servant who tries escaping. I've already sent for the slave speculator."

"Surely you're not going to sell Nat just for being off the plantation?"

"He was trying to escape, but he was also up to something else. He won't say what, so he's got to be taught a lesson. I'll finish punishing him later, then I'll sell him so far down the river that he will never have a chance to even think about escaping."

Emily realized it was useless to try reasoning with William, so she held back the words that surged through her mind.

"Another thing," William rushed on, drawing back from

★ ★

her but raising his voice again. "You are a constant source of embarrassment to me and my mother! It's bad enough that other planters suspect us of harboring a Yankee spy. . . ."

"Spy?" She laughed at the ridiculous charge. "What in the world would I spy on? I rarely go anywhere except to church, and there isn't a military camp or anything like it around here!"

"That's not the point. People have been saying that about you, and after last night, they'll say you're an abolitionist, too!"

"Why? Just because I spoke to Mrs. Yates? She was very kind to me!"

William thrust his face close to Emily's and lowered his voice but spoke with intensity. "I will not stand here and argue with you! This is the last time I will speak to you about your proper place in this home! Now, go get ready for church, or we're going to be late."

"I don't feel like going this morning."

"It's just as well. We're invited to spend the afternoon with some friends, and it would be awkward having you along. Just don't forget what I said! This is your final warning!"

As he stalked away, Emily stood where she was, her emotions churning. She sighed heavily and headed upstairs to be alone in her room.

★ ★ ★ ★ ★

Nat had not meant to cry out when the leather whip whistled and struck, lacerating his smooth back for the first time. He had tried hard to stifle the screams, but they had been torn from his throat by the worst pain he had ever felt.

It still lingered like strings of fire along his back. In agony he let his head sag against his chest while the sun played tag with darkening clouds. He had given up struggling against the leather thongs that bound him to the post. He had also given up trying to scare the flies away that buzzed around his lacerated back where he could not reach. He had only the pain and the knowledge that William would be back to finish the whipping before selling him.

He closed his eyes to encourage himself with his mother's words. *"Winning is in the mind and not the muscles."* She had told him that many times while he was growing up on the plantation where the benevolent Master Whitman didn't whip his slaves. If they were unruly, he sold them. Then he had died, and his heirs had put Nat's mother and her family up for auction.

He tried to think beyond his present misery and focus on his goal to find all of them and lead them to freedom. But he could not do that if he was sold into the deep South where escape was nearly impossible.

A soft voice roused him. "You got to run tonight."

He opened his eyes to see Sarah kneeling near him, picking up the empty wooden bucket that had held salt water. She did not look at him but whispered, "When he cuts you down, you'll hurt worse than now, but you've got to be ready to run."

"I can barely move now," he whispered.

"I know. But you must. I've got grease and black pepper hidden in a hollow log with a map of the swamp."

"The swamp?"

"Yes. I got it from one of the old woodcutters who used to work there. His master had them make a road to drain part of the swamp and bring out the timber. It's very dangerous, but it's also the safest place to hide. Nat Turner even hid out in a swamp for three years."

At Glenbury Hill where Nat had been born and lived under the benevolent Master Thaddeus Whitman, he had heard about Turner. He had also heard old woodcutters' tales of Black Water Swamp. It was a place of mystery and dread, filled with vicious biting insects, toxic water, countless animals such as bears, and poisonous reptiles such as water moccasins, copperheads, and rattlesnakes. There were many scary stories about people who

★ ★

ventured into the treacherous peat bogs and were never seen again.

"I can't talk anymore," Sarah concluded. "Be ready to run."

She left him then, never even glancing his way. Her final words echoed in his mind, reminding him again of his mother. He forced himself to stand up a little straighter in the sultry weather. *Run. Got to run.*

★ ★ ★ ★ ★

Julie was denied permission to stay home with Emily, so Emily was left alone while the rest of the family went to church.

She got up from her bed, where she had been deep in thought. She looked out the window toward the slave quarters. Nat remained where he had been left with his hands suspended over his head. Other members of his race walked by without looking at him. Emily knew that they were afraid of possible punishment if someone reported they did anything to relieve Nat's suffering.

She turned away from the sight, but the image went with her. She hurried out the door, startling the maid who had been waiting to render any service required.

Emily told Lizzie that she was going outside and hastily crossed to the kitchen building. She asked the cook, Hattie, for a sharp knife and a long-handled dipper filled with water. Hattie motioned to Sarah, the pretty teenage slave girl, who gave Emily what she wanted. She was conscious of their curious looks as she hurriedly left the kitchen with the items.

She approached Nat where he sagged against the pole under the hot and sultry summer sky. She cut his bonds, and he sank to the ground.

She held the dipper to his lips, saying, "Drink."

He raised his head and looked at her with pain-filled eyes. "He won't like this."

"I know. Go ahead, drink."

★ ★

Nat hesitated, muttered a thanks, and sipped.

When he finished, she brushed flies away from his lacerated back, but she kept her eyes averted from the wounds. She was aware that many dark eyes were watching through windows and from behind doors, but none dared come into the open to help for fear of retribution.

"I'm sorry for what he did," Emily said. "Is there someone here who will take care of your back?"

A soft voice said from behind her, "I will."

Emily turned to see Sarah approaching with a bucket of grease and a cloth in one hand. She held a long-sleeved man's shirt in the other.

Emily marveled. "You're doing a brave thing."

Sarah didn't answer but dipped the cloth in the soft grease and gently applied it to Nat's wounds.

He moaned but submitted to further application as if aware that this was the only salve available to him.

Emily asked, "Where's the older woman who usually takes care of slaves after they've been whipped?"

"Sick."

Emily felt great concern for the girl. "Here. I'll do this. You go back to the quarters before my cousin hears about this. He'll punish you for helping."

"No," Sarah said flatly. "No, he won't."

Emily didn't understand, but the girl seemed so sure of herself that Emily believed her.

Sarah finished with Nat's bare back and helped him into the shirt.

Emily wondered if it wouldn't have been better to leave the wounds exposed, but she guessed that Sarah knew something to the contrary. Turning again to Nat, Emily asked, "Can you walk?"

He nodded and used the whipping post to pull himself to his feet. "Thanks." The word was barely understandable because he spoke through lips that had cracked and dried under

★ ★

the sun, which periodically hid behind incoming storm clouds.

"Is there anything else I can do?" Emily asked.

He shook his head and winced with pain when he took the first step away from the post. Sarah draped his right arm over her shoulder to support him. Emily watched them head toward the slave quarters, where a man called Pete opened his cabin door for them.

Emily turned back toward the big house, preparing herself for the verbal abuse William would heap upon her when he returned. But she felt she had done right and was mentally ready for him.

★　★　★　★　★

Emily didn't want lunch, so she stayed in her room alone all afternoon. She half dreaded the time when William would return, yet she also welcomed it.

The mugginess inside the house combined with still air to make staying inside barely tolerable. Outside her bedchamber window, Emily saw that the clouds had begun to solidify, cutting off the sun except for brief moments. She ignored the discomfort of her clothes sticking to her and concentrated on packing her trunk.

At the sound of the carriage returning, she stepped to the window and looked down as the ornate carriage pulled by matched bay horses stopped outside the door. The moment George let the Lodge family out, William was approached by the overseer. Emily watched him gesturing toward the slave quarters before William looked up at her window. She did not flinch but steadily met his furious eyes.

He stormed into her room without knocking. His sister followed him in, her face tear-stained.

"Please, William!" she pleaded. "Don't!"

The first lightning flash lit up the room as he strode up to Emily, his face as dark as the blackening sky. "How dare you?" he roared. "It hasn't been four hours since I warned you not to interfere in my business, but you didn't listen!"

Emily waited silently while he continued. "My mother and I gave you everything when you had nothing! We tried to put up with your stupid Yankee ideas, but you never learned to keep your place! You are a disgrace to our family!"

It was a temptation to defend herself, but Emily had mentally retreated to a place of quiet peace that she had done the right thing by Nat.

Julie pleaded, "William, please don't—"

"Shut up!" Her brother whirled to face her, his face livid. "I run this place while our father's away!"

The door opened quickly and his mother stuck her head in. "William, come quickly. A field hand just reported that Nat and a girl named Sarah ran away."

"What?" William roared. When his mother silently nodded, he spun again to face Emily. "When I get back, I want you out of here! Take that abolitionist woman's offer! You be on that wagon tomorrow morning, and don't ever let me see you around here again!"

Julie let out a little scream. "No, William! Don't let it end like this!"

He spun to glower at her. "You want to go with her?" When Julie lowered her eyes, he rushed toward the door. "Emily," he growled over his shoulder, "you're the most ungrateful person I've ever known. I hope you suffer plenty for the terrible wrong you've done!"

Julie threw her arms around Emily and wept brokenly while the sound of William's heavy footsteps faded away down the hallway toward the stairs. Another flash of lightning brilliantly lit the room. The crash of thunder shook the house.

"My plan worked!" she joyfully whispered to herself. "I'm going home!"

★ ★ ★ ★ ★

★ ★

The hot, muggy weather grew ominously still at dusk when Gideon started to recognize landmarks. "We're almost home," he told Hercules, "and no sign of Odell." The jagged lightning streaks were dangerously close and getting closer. Glancing apprehensively at the blackened sky, he knew the danger of a rider being struck and killed. It had happened to an old villager whose horse had three of its shoes knocked loose, yet the animal lived.

Would Odell stay in the saddle, or would he seek shelter? Was it worth Gideon's risking his life to keep riding in a final effort to catch up to the thief?

As the boy debated, sheet lightning lit up the sky and the land. Just ahead, entering a stand of trees, Gideon saw a man dismounting. Gideon ducked low in the saddle before thunder crashed and darkness fell again. Gideon frowned. *That looks like a soldier, not Odell!* Scowling, Gideon was suddenly concerned that he had never positively identified Odell on this trip. Both Isham and Gideon had believed they were on Odell's trail, yet there was no definite proof of that. *Could I have been following the wrong man?*

With a groan of disappointment, Gideon stopped the mule and got down. *Well, if it is Odell, he's almost home. But he's probably looking for shelter until the lightning stops. There's only one way to be sure if it's Odell—get close enough to see his face.*

It would soon be dark enough to do that, so Gideon led Hercules into the trees and picketed him fifty yards from the man. Gideon slipped from tree to tree until he was close enough to observe his quarry without being seen. There Gideon crouched in a bush that gave scant shelter from the rain, but was safer than staying by a tree, which might be struck. Then Gideon waited.

★ ★ ★ ★ ★

Twilight still provided enough visibility for Nat and Sarah

★ ★

to see their way as they ran among the trees along the river bottom. The first drops of rain soaked through Nat's borrowed shirt and into his fresh whip wounds. His face contorted in agony, but he kept running, knowing the penalty for failing to escape.

Sarah puffed, "I wish we could have waited for full darkness, but at least the rain will wash away our scent so the dogs can't follow us. Just keep well back in these trees so the patrollers don't see us until we get to the swamp."

Nat hurt too much to talk, so he bobbed his head. Pain was only part of the price he knew must be paid for the hope of reaching freedom, so he struggled on beside Sarah.

She told him, "When I ran away before, it wasn't raining, and I got caught with Pete. When the rain stops, the dogs will try to pick up our scent. So don't put on the grease and pepper until then."

Glancing around as if to check landmarks unknown to Nat, Sarah added, "I've tried to memorize the map so if it's too dark to see, we should still be able to find our way. But we have to be at the pick-up point by dawn tomorrow or we'll miss our ride. They can't risk waiting for us if we're late."

"Who're they?" Nat asked.

"I wasn't told so that if we're caught, they can't whip any names out of me. Don't lose that bed sheet." Sarah motioned toward where it was wetly wrapped around the containers of grease and black pepper stuck inside Nat's waistband. "White patrollers are as afraid of ghosts as most of our people."

Lightning split the sky, momentarily driving away the hulking black shapes that marked the trees along the river. As the thunder faded, Nat asked, "Ghosts?"

"I learned a lot since getting caught before," she said. "That's why I slipped the sheet out of the white folks' laundry one day and hid it for now."

It occurred to Nat that Sarah had also somehow convinced someone to let her move from the fields into the kitchen, where pepper and grease were kept. George must have had a hand in that as well as giving her details that went into making the map.

The sky flared up again. Sarah said, "We're passing the Tugwell farm. The swamp is not far now."

Nat nodded but didn't reply. Every step seemed to make his wounds hurt more so that he desperately wished he could rest. But a mental image of what would happen if they were caught kept him moving.

"Just ahead," Sarah said after the next lightning flash, "we have to turn into the swamp." She paused, then added, "I would rather die in there than go back."

Nat brushed drops of water from his eyebrows and looked questioningly at her.

She explained, "My mama was whipped to death when I was little. If I got caught now, young Master William might do the same to me. Even if he let me live, he'd make me 'jump the broom' with Julius. He's so mean that I'd rather die in the swamp than have to be with him."

Nat believed her, although he didn't intend to lose his life. He followed Sarah into the swamp where others had gotten lost and were never seen again.

SURPRISE!
SURPRISE!

The storm's darkness made the early evening seem later than it was as Gideon waited for an opportunity to find out if he had followed Odell or a stranger.

The boy stayed hunched over in the underbrush, away from the nearest tree but close enough that he could watch the man a few yards away. The warm summer rain soaked Gideon's clothes in spite of his efforts to make a shelter of his blanket. It was as wet as he, making him more miserable. He had not risked a fire, which would betray his presence, although the man he followed had unsuccessfully tried to make a campfire in the rain.

Gideon's concern grew every time a flash of lightning showed more clearly that the man seemed to be a Confederate soldier. He sat with his back against a log wearing a slouch hat, which many Confederates preferred to the regulation headgear. His gray Richmond jacket was standard, but was he really a soldier?

Gideon had seen similar ones abandoned on the plains at Manassas along with other accoutrements, such as canteens, haversacks, and other personal items. Guns were in such short supply that these had all been picked up by victorious Southerners.

Gideon berated himself as the darkness deepened. *How can*

I go home if I've been following the wrong man and I let Odell get away with Papa's money?

The sky lit up less explosively and the roll of thunder passed before Gideon felt it was safe to slip over for a closer look at his solitary neighbor.

In case it was Odell and Gideon managed to recover the gold, he decided it would be best to take two precautions. He saddled Hercules and tied the wet blanket in place, then double-checked to make sure that the mule was securely tied to a stout shrub, ready to mount and ride hard toward home. If the man was Odell, Gideon planned to delay any pursuit by freeing Odell's horse and running it off so it would take time to catch.

But before I do that, Gideon warned himself, *I've got to be absolutely sure who that man is. If he's a soldier, he might shoot me for trying to steal his horse.*

Satisfied with his plan, Gideon bent low and cautiously slipped through the brush toward the unsuspecting man sitting with his back against a log fifty yards away.

Gideon needed the occasional lightning flashes to see the man's face, so he crawled on hands and knees in the mud and sodden leaves until he was close. Each time light flickered across the sky, Gideon froze, then eased on during the following darkness.

When he was as close as necessary, Gideon waited until lightning chased the shadows away and the man's face was clearly visible. *It is Odell! Now let's see if my plan works to get Papa's money back.*

Crawling away, Gideon circled around to where the thief's horse was picketed. When Gideon slowly stood up by the horse, it nickered softly with ears pointed to the boy. Quietly, gently, Gideon reached for the bridle and untied the picket rope. The animal blew noisily while Gideon turned him to face away from where Hercules was hidden.

When lightning again illuminated the sky, Gideon released

★ ★

the halter, then slapped the horse's wet near hindquarter with all his strength. The animal neighed loudly and noisily plunged off through the trees.

Gideon crouched low, barely hearing the man's surprised shout. He leaped up and ran after the horse.

Having already carefully marked his course by earlier lightning flashes, Gideon dashed toward the spot where the man had been resting. Gideon reached for the saddlebags he had seen earlier hanging over a bush.

"The gold is too heavy to carry in his pockets," Gideon muttered as his muddy fingers explored the saddlebags in the darkness, "so it's got to be in something like these."

A few seconds of futile fumbling upset Gideon. *It's not here!* He paused to make sure that he could still hear the man chasing after his horse. *So where is it?* He risked standing and took a step in the dark where he stumbled over a blanket.

He fell, his hands landing on something he guessed was a cartridge box. *Not that, either!* He scrambled to a crouching position so he would be less visible by the next lightning streak, then sent his muddy fingers exploring over the wet ground.

He touched what felt like a percussion cap pouch, then a canteen. *They're not in these.* He muttered desperately, "Maybe he's got a haversack or knapsack."

His exploring fingers touched a haversack with the strap to carry it over a shoulder. It was empty. The canvas knapsack with straps for wearing it on the back was filled with personal belongings. There was a deck of cards, a pipe and tobacco pouch, but no coins.

Gideon dropped the knapsack and glanced into the night. He heard the man's voice and the horse's soft whickering, indicating the animal had been caught. *He'll be coming back. I don't dare search any longer!*

Gideon stood up and pivoted on the muddy ground. Something clinked musically at his feet. Instantly, he knelt, feeling

★ ★

along the bottom of the log where the man had been sitting. Gideon's fingers closed over a small, heavy coin.

"Papa's gold!" he whispered, shoving the coin into his pocket. Frantically, knowing the man was returning, Gideon felt in the darkness, finding more coins. He guessed that Odell had been playing with them and dropped them when the horse ran away. *He was probably doing the same thing on horseback when he threw away Papa's handkerchief. Where are the rest of these coins?*

Gideon desperately raked his fingers along the muddy ground, joyfully counting each coin before shoving them into his pockets. *Eleven, twelve . . . should be one more.* He felt again in the mud. *I can't find it, and I don't dare wait any . . . whoops! Thirteen!*

Rising only enough to be able to run, Gideon gripped his front pockets with both hands so the coins would make less sound. He ran, almost doubled over, darting through the brush, instantly stopping when lightning flashed. He was greatly relieved that there was no shout behind him.

Leaping into the saddle, he grasped the reins and leaned low over the mule's mane. "Pick up your feet, Hercules," he whispered. "Let's ease out of here!"

The thudding of his heart seemed as loud as the receding thunder when he reached the end of the tree line. There still was no howl of discovery from behind. Gideon glanced back at the next flash, but the trees cut off his vision. He faced forward again, flinching at the noisy sucking sound Hercules' hooves made each time he lifted them from the mud.

At the same time Gideon felt elated. *I would like to see Odell's face when he tries to convince Cobb that Papa's money just disappeared in the middle of the night. Cobb will think Odell wants to keep all the gold for himself, and I have a feeling Cobb won't be nice!*

Gideon almost chuckled at the thought but knew it was too soon to feel confident. He was almost home, but if Odell figured out what had really happened, he could catch Gideon before he reached the farm.

He was surprised when a distant lightning flash revealed several mounted soldiers riding toward him.

"Halt!" The command and ominous sound of weapons being cocked stopped Gideon instantly. His heart sank when he was quickly surrounded in the darkness.

★　★　★　★　★

One of the last flashes of lightning overwhelmed the coal-oil lamp burning in Emily's room, where she and Julie sat in grief-stricken silence on the edge of the bed. The following thunder sounded late and far away.

"Our last night together," Julie said, a catch in her voice. "I'm going to miss you so terribly much!"

"I'll miss you, too." Emily had a difficult time keeping her own voice steady. "But we'll meet again."

"Maybe not in this life."

Sliding an arm around her cousin, Emily tried to sound confident. "Of course we will! The war won't last forever, so we'll get together again lots of times."

"I wish I could be sure of that."

"You have to have faith." Emily dropped her arm and walked over to the window. "Faith, like knowing this storm is about over and the sun will shine again tomorrow. Oh, look! The full moon is already showing through the last of those clouds."

Emily opened the window. "Everything always smells so fresh and clean after a rain."

Julie came to stand beside her and sniffed the air. "You'll have a slow trip tomorrow in a wagon because the roads will be so muddy."

"I don't mind, just as long as I get to Richmond and then on to Illinois." She sighed, adding, "I just wish I could have said good-bye to Gideon, but I guess he's still not back from going to see his brother."

"I guess not."

"Listen!" Emily exclaimed. "What's that?"

Julie cocked her head. "Just some hounds starting to bay on a scent."

Breathlessly, Emily asked, "You mean Nat and Sarah?"

Slowly, Julie nodded. "The dogs couldn't follow them in the rain, but now that it's stopped . . ."

"Don't say it!" Emily exclaimed, quickly laying a restraining hand on the other girl's arm.

Julie quickly closed the window, but the baying of the hounds drifted into the room.

"I wonder how long before the dogs find the scent?" Emily looked at Julie, who shrugged. Emily shuddered, knowing that she could not do a thing to help the fugitives.

★　★　★　★　★

After the command to halt, Gideon didn't move.

The full moon sailed majestically from behind one of the last of the storm clouds, showing him that two troopers had grabbed Hercules' bridle from either side so he couldn't run. The moon also revealed that all of the horsemen surrounding him were Confederates.

"Who are you?" one of them on the right demanded.

The boy relaxed slightly. "I'm Gideon Tugwell from Church Creek, which is just ahead a short ways."

"You're soaked. Why're you out here in the rain?"

"I've been to see my brother who was wounded at Manassas. I'm going home to tell my folks." Gideon didn't feel it was necessary to mention anything else.

"How old are you?"

"I'll be thirteen in October."

"Do you know that some boys your age are fighting in this war?"

"Yes, but my father is sick, and I'm the oldest boy at home, so . . ."

"Never mind. We're looking for a deserter. Have you seen anyone who looks suspicious?"

Gideon started to shake his head, then stopped. "Well, I don't know about any deserter, but right back there in those trees behind me, there's a fellow dressed sort of like you are."

An understanding look quickly passed among the troopers. "Thanks," the spokesman said, then turned his horse toward the trees.

Gideon watched the others fall in behind him. "Hercules," he whispered, "now I think we can safely reach home."

★　★　★　★　★

When Gideon smelled the swamp, he also heard hounds running there, but he didn't care. Home was just a short distance away. He urged Hercules to a faster pace, anticipating the joy of seeing his family, giving Papa the gold, plus changing into dry clothes and having a hot meal. It sounded wonderful, except for one terrible problem: *How can I tell them about Isham?*

A mule's raucous bray startled Gideon. He glanced ahead to where some trees cast moon shadows on the road. Gideon's immediate thought was that Odell had eluded his Confederate captors and beaten him home, but that wasn't logical.

The rider ahead emerged from the shadows and twisted in the saddle to look back. The moonlight fell fully on his face.

Gideon let out a whoop. "Isham!"

"Gideon?" The surprised cry was like an echo.

"Yes! Yes!" Gideon kicked Hercules in the ribs and slapped the ends of the reins lightly along his shoulders and galloped to meet his brother.

After a brief but joyful reunion, the brothers laughingly agreed on how they would make their appearance at home. Gideon rode on ahead, his coming trumpeted by the family hounds. They followed him back down the lane to the house while Isham stayed out of sight by the public road.

Gideon's wet clothes clung to his body, and there was mud on everything except the palms of his hands where he had wiped them off on Hercules' mane. But he had never felt so proud and happy when his mother and Ben opened the door to see why the dogs were barking.

"Gideon!" Ben yelled. "Papa! Girls! It's Gideon!"

In seconds Mother, Ben, Kate, and Lilly were all trying to hug him at once, shouting to their father, who slowly shuffled to the door. He stopped, looking old and tired.

"Hello, Papa," Gideon said, gently freeing himself from a tangle of arms and going inside to stand in front of him. "I brought you something."

Reaching into both front pockets, Gideon pulled out double handfuls of yellow coins. They were muddy but excitingly beautiful.

"Thirteen of them," he said quietly, extending them to his father. "Two hundred and sixty dollars."

There were *ohs* and *ahs* from everyone except Papa. He said nothing as Gideon slowly poured the coins into his open palms. Gideon waited, watching his face and ignoring the excited questions bursting from everyone else's lips.

Tears glistened in Papa's eyes as he lifted them to look fully into Gideon's own. "Son, do you remember when I said that you couldn't do anything right?"

Yes, many times, Gideon thought, then checked himself. "Yes, Papa."

"I was very wrong." With the coins gripped in his hands, he threw both arms around Gideon's neck. "I . . . I did you wrong, son." Papa's voice cracked when he added, "I'm so sorry, son!" He began to sob brokenly.

The house was suddenly quiet except for some sniffling by those surrounding father and son.

Gideon waited until his father's body quit shaking before

★ ★

whispering, "It's all right, Papa. Really."

Very gently, he added, "I've got another surprise for you; for all of you."

His father released him and stepped back, looking down at the coins in his hands. "You saw Isham?"

"Yes. He was wounded, but he's all right."

"We heard," Mrs. Tugwell said. "Some nice woman wrote us because his right arm was hurt. How is he?"

All eyes turned expectantly to Gideon. "Well," he said, drawing out the word. "Why don't you . . ." He left the question unfinished and stepped to the door. Opening it with a flourish, he concluded happily, ". . . ask him yourselves?"

Mother and younger children rushed by Gideon to throw their arms around the older brother who stood grinning in the open doorway, trying to hug back with his good arm and protect his right arm in its sling.

When things had quieted down, the girls sat on Isham's lap. Ben leaned on Gideon's knee, and their mother stood by her husband's chair with her hand lightly resting on his shoulder.

"So," Isham concluded, "when I told those Yankees where I was from, this one trooper got all excited. He said, 'Do you know a girl named Emily Lodge who lives near there?'

"I told him, 'She's a friend of my younger brother. Why do you ask?'

"He said, 'She's my little sister's best friend back in Illinois. My sister's name is Jessie Barlow; I'm Brice.'

" 'No!' I said to him, not really believing it.

" 'As God is my witness,' Brice Barlow told me. 'I ran into her very briefly the other day when we rode through your area. She's grown since I last saw her.' "

Isham looked around at each person in turn, making them eagerly howl for him to go on.

Kate, always the practical one, asked, "How did you get away from them?"

Gideon had briefly heard about that when he and Isham

met on the road, but Gideon waited eagerly to hear it again.

"Strange thing about that," Isham finally explained, frowning. "They got careless and wandered off together, leaving me alone. Untied. With the mule I had borrowed from Carolyn's father saddled nearby."

"You escaped!" Ben shouted, clapping his hands. "Good for you!"

Gideon met Isham's eyes and realized that there was more to the story than that. *They let him get away! I hope that doesn't get them in trouble. But it was sure a nice thing to do.*

"Wait until I tell Emily," Gideon said. At the look on Ben's face, he asked, "Unless she's already gone?"

"I saw her down in the river bottom the other day," Ben explained. "She was planning on leaving soon. Maybe she's already gone."

Gideon felt an emotion he couldn't explain creep over him. He took a slow, deep breath, his mind racing.

Papa said, "You boys had better get into some dry clothes." He turned to his wife. "Martha, I imagine they could eat a bite if it was offered."

"Oh, of course!" She leaped up. "I've got some good leftovers. Kate! Lilly! You set the table. Ben, help them find dry clothes!"

Gideon lingered, stopping by his father's chair. "Papa," he said, looking tenderly down at the tired face. "Now you can have the medicine you need to get well."

His father slowly stood, facing him. "I don't say some things very often, but, well, you make me proud."

His voice broke and he pushed past Gideon, opened the door, and stepped out onto the porch. Gideon looked at his mother.

"He's never let his children see him cry," she whispered. "He needs a few minutes alone."

Gideon nodded and started to follow Isham and Ben when a strange thump came from outside. He glanced at his mother,

★ ★

but she was already running for the door, wiping her hands on the apron.

The kerosene lamp's pale yellow glow showed Papa collapsed on the porch.

Gideon was aware of his mother's scream, and the rest of the family rushed through the small house to join them. Gideon's mother frantically called his father's name, but he didn't move.

Gideon couldn't, either. He stood transfixed, not understanding, until Isham bent over and took his father's limp wrist. He held it for several seconds as a terrible fear gripped Gideon.

Isham slowly raised his face to the others. His voice was a hoarse whisper. "He's dead."

A DAWN OF
CHANGE

The full moon slowly broke through the storm clouds as the rain passed over the swamp. Nat and Sarah kept running, splashing through puddles left by the rain or struggling to keep from falling on soft, miry ground that shook underfoot or sucked at their feet.

"Now that the rain's stopped, we had better put on the grease and black pepper and hope the hounds don't pick up our trail," Sarah suggested.

"I would think that the man following us would have quit and gone home when the rain fell so hard."

Sarah gingerly checked a soggy downed log to be sure there was no snake on it before she sat down. Once that night she had almost stepped on a poisonous cottonmouth snake. A warning flash of white in the open mouth had alerted her, and she had avoided being bitten.

"You don't know Barley Cobb," Sarah said. "They say he hates our people so much he never quits. He also charges a white owner plenty for catching a runaway. You're probably worth a hundred and fifty dollars because you're a skilled body slave. I'm only a kitchen helper, so a reward for me is maybe fifty dollars."

She held out her hand. "Please let me have that tablecloth with the grease and pepper wrapped in it."

Nat handed it over. He was near exhaustion, and the rain-soaked shirt made the open wounds on his back hurt worse. He asked, "Does pepper and grease really work?"

"It's supposed to, but I never heard for sure."

Sarah wiped as much mud and leaves off her legs as possible before beginning to apply the kitchen grease. She started sneezing from the pepper. The sound seemed unusually loud in the swamp's hushed vastness.

Nat turned away and pressed the back of his forefinger hard between his nostrils and upper lip in hopes he would not sneeze. He didn't. Relieved, he looked back on their trail. The shadows were so dense, all he could see were strange, ghostly wisps silently rising from the thick undergrowth that vanished into the tree canopy. Knowing that the swamp was filled with many creatures made the silence more ominous.

Nat said anxiously, "We need to be going."

"I'm almost finished. Here. You start with the grease while I put the pepper on my feet. The grease helps hold the pepper. Save part of it. We might need to throw it in the hounds' eyes if they catch us. I'll keep the tablecloth in case we need it for something."

Nat sat down beside Sarah and began applying the messy grease to his shoes and legs. Anxious eyes sought the sky again. "Daylight is coming fast. We'll have to hurry to get to the pickup point before then."

"I know. The conductor can't wait if we're late. Even white abolitionists don't want to be seen doing something suspicious, like waiting near this swamp."

"I'm ready." Nat stood up. "How much farther to the road?"

"Should be close." She took a few steps, then gasped and leaped back, bumping into Nat. "Oh!"

"What is it?" Nat stepped up beside her, then stopped and gulped. A shaft of moonlight through the trees fell on a human skull half buried in the soil.

For a moment both stood in silence before Nat said quietly, "I've heard stories from old woodcutters about people who got lost in here and were never seen again. Sometimes only their bones were found. There's something in the peat that helps preserve them. Let's go around and keep moving."

Nat cast an anxious eye to the sky, now showing the first hint of approaching dawn. "How much farther?"

Sarah took a couple of deep breaths before saying, "According to the map, we should have come to a corduroy road by now."

Nat felt a tingle of concern. "Are you saying we're lost?"

"I hope not."

Nat stopped dead still, the mud sucking at his feet. "Are you serious?"

"Well, I've never been here any more than you have, and this map that George got from an old woodcutter may not be right."

"We're running out of time." Nat tried to keep the fear from his tone. "If we miss that wagon, there won't be another, and we can't go back to Briarstone."

Sarah looked at Nat with piercing dark eyes. "I would rather die here than ever go back."

"Don't say that! I'm not willing to die here!"

He cast an anxious glance all around, hoping to see some sign of the ditch while a rising sense of desperation gripped him. "My mother used to tell me that winning was in the mind and not the muscles. We have to control our fear and use our heads. Come on."

He clutched her free hand and half pulled her with him. His eyes probed everywhere for some sign of hope. In a few minutes the brush unexpectedly ended and a wide-open area spread before them. In the moonlight a straight stretch along the ground seemed out of place in the irregular, tangled undergrowth.

"That's it!" Sarah exclaimed, dropping his hand and pointing. "The road! We follow this to where the ditch was cut to

★ ★

drain this place. It leads to the swamp's edge where we'll be picked up."

"Let's go! Daylight is almost here!"

It was somewhat easier running over the log road. Years ago, logs had been laid side by side along higher ground where rising waters were less likely to reach. Heavy undergrowth had since reclaimed part of the road so that the fugitives were scratched by thorny vines and devil's walking-stick plants. This frequently forced Nat and Sarah off the road onto spongy peat made by generations of decaying vegetation.

"We're going to make it!" Sarah cried. "We're going to—" She was interrupted by the baying of hounds suddenly behind them. "We put the grease and pepper on too late! They've got our scent!"

"They're close!" Nat grabbed her hand again and began running. "They're coming real fast!"

★　★　★　★　★

Emily slept fitfully and awoke at the distant sound of the day horn calling slaves to get up and labor in the tobacco fields. Her head ached as much as her heart as she slid down out of the high bed, lit the kerosene lamp, and recoiled at her image in the mirror.

"You look frightful!" she whispered. Her father had once described her long gold hair as spun strands of sunshine, but now it was loose and tousled from endless tossing and turning. Her unique violet eyes were dull with dark circles under them.

"What have you done?" she murmured to herself. "You're only twelve, and you're leaving the only living relatives you have to try getting back to Illinois. Even if you get there, how will you live? You can't expect Jessie and her family to support you."

The door opened quietly, and Julie, in her long nightgown, stuck her head in. "Who're you talking to?" Emily hurried across to throw her arms around her cousin. "Myself. I was just having second thoughts."

For a moment the girls silently clung to each other, sharing the agony of parting, perhaps forever.

"Well," Emily said, breaking away and wiping a tear from her cheek with her forefinger. "I'm all packed except for changing out of these nightclothes into my traveling ones. I want to be downstairs when Mr. Yates gets here so he doesn't have to wait."

"Will you be all right?"

"Yes, with God's help. I've prayed so hard about this that I'm sure it's the right thing even though my fear is now trying to overcome my faith."

"We'll write to each other," Julie said as Emily stepped into the closet to change. "Even though the mail isn't running between North and South, I've heard that some private parties who have passes will carry letters across Union lines for a price."

"I left my address at Jessie's there by the lamp." Emily emerged buttoning a basic outfit of gathered bodice with white collar and cuffs. It would be cooler in the humid climate and protect her arms from the sun.

To avoid possibly breaking down and crying, she changed the subject and tried to sound cheerful. "I'm going to wear my wide-brimmed hat because there won't be a roof on Mr. Yates's farm wagon," Emily mused as she approached the mirror to straighten her clothes.

"That outfit looks very drab," Julie said. "You need something prettier, more cheerful." She reached into the top dresser drawer and produced a pink ribbon. "Here. Pull your hair back and tie it with this. You'll be cooler with the hair off your neck, too."

When both girls were dressed, they went downstairs while two male house servants carried Emily's small trunk out to the front porch. The first hint of dawn touched the Confederate

★ ★

flag attached to one of the glistening white Corinthian pillars. A clink of trace chains and squeak of leather on a draft horse's harness proved that the wagon had started up the long drive from the road toward the house.

With wide-brimmed hat in hand, Emily expectantly looked back at the massive front door now closed. She heard Julie give an embarrassed cough.

"Mama is having one of her sick spells and asked to be excused," she said, not looking at Emily. "My brother had to leave early with the overseer. They asked me to say good-bye for them."

"I understand." Emily truly did, but she felt hurt that her parting was under such trying circumstances.

"Hello, girls," the older driver said, reining in his team of heavy draft horses. "Emily, I haven't had a chance to meet you, but you have met my wife, Clara."

They acknowledged that while the two housemen slid the trunk onto the wagon's tailgate and behind rows of potted young peach trees. The girls tried to hold back the tears, but they slid down their cheeks as the cousins hugged and said good-bye.

Mr. Yates helped Emily up to sit beside him on the high, open seat at the front of the wagon, then gathered the reins in his hands.

Emily had to struggle to keep her voice steady as she looked down at Julie. "I guess I'm not going to see my friend Gideon. Well, good-bye, Julie. Write me."

"I will. Bye."

The driver clucked to the team, and the wagon began to roll. It followed the circular drive around and back down the lane under the line of trees toward the road. Emily took one last look at Julie through eyes misted with tears. Then she resolutely faced toward the dawn.

★ ★ ★ ★ ★

★ ★

For most of the night, Gideon had kept a death watch with his tearful family at the bedside where his father's body lay. Gideon whispered brokenly, "I can't believe he's dead! Not after he's got the money for his medicine and Isham is home! He can't be!"

Others occasionally voiced the same denial, but the still form on the bed proved them wrong.

At last, at his mother's insistence, Gideon and his siblings had gone to bed. But sleep wouldn't come to Gideon. His mind whirled with a thousand thoughts until he could not stand staying inside anymore.

He tried to roll out of his narrow bed without bothering his brothers, but Isham was awake.

"Where you going?" he whispered in the darkness.

Gideon pulled on dry clothes by the first light of the coming day. "To think."

"Want company?"

"If you don't mind, I'd like to be alone."

"I understand." Isham's voice held a slight tremor as he lay back down. "Little brother, you did a great job all by yourself. Papa was proud of you. Me too."

Gideon's eyes filled with tears. "Thanks. But he's dead, and I'm so sick at heart that I can't stand it."

"You must, and you will. I'll have to go back to Camp Pickens in a few days. I can try to get a hardship discharge, but even if I do, it'll take time. You will have a terribly big responsibility on your shoulders, but you can handle it. You've already proven you can."

Gideon reached out and squeezed Isham's good hand hard. "Why did he have to die, especially like this and especially now?"

"I wish I knew."

Ben stirred slightly in his bed as the older brothers' voices rose.

"I've got to go," Gideon said. He released his brother's

★ ★

hand, felt for his pencil and paper, then made his way on silent bare feet through the house. His parents' bedroom door was closed. Gideon imagined his mother asleep in her chair by the bed, where her husband lay so silent and still.

Outside on the porch, with the two family hounds pressing around him for attention, Gideon pulled on his shoes but didn't speak to the dogs. He lit the lantern and carried it with his pencil and paper to the barn.

The fragrance of hay and the warm smell of the two mules and the family milk cow greeted him. He hung the lantern on a nail and climbed into the hay where he planned to try writing some of the swirling emotions and thoughts that tore at his heart.

But he could not write. Instead, his head dropped upon his knees, and tears splattered upon the paper. "Oh, Papa! Papa!" he whispered. "Why did you have to die?"

He didn't know how long he stayed there, racked by grief, but he heard the roosters start crowing from the chicken roosts behind the barn. Vaguely, somewhere in the back of his mind, he faintly heard the plodding of horses' hooves on the public road. The trace chains jingled and the wheels made a faint noise as they turned up the dust. Gideon did not look up.

★　★　★　★　★

Emily found that Mr. Yates tended to drive in silence, but she didn't mind. She sat beside him on the wagon seat with the young peach trees making slight swishing sounds as they bounced from the rough road.

She ached for Julie and the hardships she had to endure in a household where she was the only gentle one. Emily also hurt emotionally because she had not seen Gideon since she had started to tell him about seeing Brice. Gideon had suddenly ridden off, saying someone was following him. She wished she could have clarified what he meant.

Emily was so deep in meditation that she was not aware of

★　★

where she was until dogs barked back off the road. She looked that direction and realized those were the Tugwells' two hounds.

Gideon, where are you? Your house is dark. Hmm? That's strange. Farmers are always up by dawn. I hope nothing's happened!

She shook off that thought. *I guess he's still not back, so I'll never see him again.*

Mr. Yates lightly slapped the reins along the backs of his team, and the wagon rolled slowly by.

Emily twisted in the seat for another look at the Tugwell place. Then she sighed and again resolutely faced forward. The only sound besides the team and wagon was the baying of hounds following a trail somewhere in the swamp that lay ahead.

Suddenly, Mr. Yates stiffened and cocked his head to listen. "Those are Barley Cobb's dogs," he said so softly as if almost talking only to himself.

Emily roused herself from her own reveries. "How do you know?"

"Hear that one with the choppy voice? It's not the way most hounds bay on a trail, so I can recognize that one as belonging to Cobb."

Emily sensed something unspoken in the man's tone. "Is he chasing some runaway slave?"

For a moment he didn't answer. Finally, he nodded. "Maybe two." He slapped the reins hard against the plodding draft horses. "Giddyap there!"

Emily was surprised as the team began a faster pace. At the same time she had a sudden, terrible feeling. "Is there something I should know?"

"I was going to wait until the right time to tell you, but maybe you should know now. We're going to have a couple of fugitive slaves as hidden passengers."

Emily gasped. "Isn't that very dangerous?"

★ ★

"Yes, if we're caught. But it will be worse for those poor souls in the swamp running from those dogs."

Emily glanced toward the swamp shrouded in mist. *Nat and Sarah!* The names exploded in her mind. *They must be running for their lives!*

THE SWAMP GHOST

Still grieving alone in the barn's hayloft, Gideon was vaguely aware of the stamping of the mules' hooves and lowing by the cow. Knowing they were hungry and the cow needed to be milked, Gideon sighed and raised his head. He hadn't written a word in his journal.

He stood up, folded the blank sheet of paper, and stuck it in his shirt pocket with the pencil stub. He reached for the pitchfork to throw down hay to the manger but stopped with the fork in midair.

Frowning, he recalled hearing the sound of a heavy farm wagon and draft team passing along the public road a short time before. *Could that have been Emily leaving on her trip?*

For a moment he debated the logic of that. *Probably not. But what if it is? Should I go see?*

He also considered the propriety of riding off to possibly say good-bye to her while leaving his family in this time of grief and shock. He decided, *I'll go and be back before anyone here is up.*

He jabbed the fork tines into the hay, slid down, and jumped over the manger. In one quick motion he lifted the bridle from its wall peg and approached Hercules. "Sorry," he said soothingly, "I know you're still tired and you're hungry, but this can't wait."

When the bit was in place in the mule's mouth, Gideon took

the reins and led Hercules to the barn door. Shoving it open, he saw that the morning sky had lightened a lot since he had gotten up.

"No time for the saddle," he mused and swung up on the mule's bare back. Clucking with his tongue and tapping sharply with his heels along the flanks, he said, "Let's see if we can catch up to that wagon to see if Emily is on it."

★ ★ ★ ★ ★

Emily clearly heard hounds baying on a hot trail when Mr. Yates turned the team off the road. A faint trail led across the field adjacent toward the swamp. "Where are we going?" she asked.

"To get our passengers if they get to the pick-up point on time."

Emily was sure that Mr. Yates was an abolitionist helping with the Underground Railroad. She said, "I had heard that slaves are only helped to escape at night."

"They usually are, but we're going to try this way and see how it works. After we're well away from here tonight, we'll transfer them to someone else for the second leg of their escape. It will be harder for them to be traced, and you and I can breathe easier."

Emily glanced back at the wagon bed loaded with her trunk and little peach trees. "There's no room."

"It's supposed to look that way, but actually there are two separate hiding places. A smaller one is under our seat, and a longer one concealed behind us. Each compartment has drinking water and air holes for the fugitives. It will be hot and dusty, but safe."

He turned to look toward the swamp. "Now, let's hope they don't get caught before they get to the pick-up point. Once they're safely hidden and their scent is off the ground, the hounds can't trail them."

Emily listened apprehensively to the dogs and the whooping of a man urging them on. "What happens if the dogs catch them before they reach us?"

When Mr. Yates didn't answer, Emily realized the awful truth. He was not armed, and there was nothing that could be done. The thought made her shiver. Then another shudder shook her as she realized what could also happen to her and Mr. Yates if Cobb saw them drive off with the two fugitive slaves.

★ ★ ★ ★ ★

Nat and Sarah panted through the swamp, trying to beat the dawn and the slave catcher's hounds that were closing in on them from behind. Nearing exhaustion and breathing hard, the couple ran and staggered along the rough corduroy road. The old logs, laid side by side, made treacherous footing. The vines that overgrew the road tore their skin and clothes or slapped them in the face with stinging force.

Nat reached inside his soaked shirt and brought out what was left of the can of black pepper. "It's not the dogs' fault, but if it comes down to them or us, I'll have to throw this in their faces. Then maybe we can reach the pick-up point before Cobb catches up to us."

"I haven't heard him hollering lately," Sarah panted. "Do you suppose he's circled around and is trying to head us off?"

"I hadn't thought of that. But he must know about this road and figure we can run faster on it than on the muddy swamp ground." Nat glanced back as the baying hounds burst into view, charging hard, their long ears flopping, vicious teeth showing.

"You keep going," Nat ordered, stopping and taking the lid off the can of pepper. "Let's hope this works!"

Sarah staggered on, the wet tablecloth trailing from her hand.

It took all of Nat's willpower to wait until the two hounds were almost upon him. They rushed shoulder to shoulder along the log road, their cries changing to the triumphant "treed" bark as they prepared for a final leap upon their hapless victim.

"Now!" Nat cried, throwing the remaining black pepper into the open mouths and eyes.

For a split second he thought it hadn't worked, then the dogs yelped in surprise and pain. They spun away, vigorously flopping their long ears and trying to shake off the powder. They sneezed, bawled loudly, and plunged into the underbrush. There they thrashed wildly about before running off into the distance, their whining marking their retreat.

"It worked, Sarah! Wait for me!" As fast as he could, he ran after her along the slippery log road. He quickly caught up with her.

Sarah happily announced, "We're not lost! There's the ditch, and our meeting place should be close by!"

"Great! But we don't have much time." He grabbed Sarah's hand, and they ran on together.

She panted, "I wonder where Cobb is? Why don't we hear him calling to his dogs, especially since they're not baying on our trail anymore?"

"Who knows? Listen!" Nat didn't stop but strained to hear better. "I think I hear a team and wagon up ahead and to the right. Hear it?"

"Yes." Sarah was panting hard and staggering more with fatigue. "They're coming for us."

Nat dodged a thorny vine that snagged his long-sleeved shirt. "How long will they wait?"

"Not long, I was told. We should be almost there."

Nat tried to increase his pace but tripped over a trailing vine and fell headlong onto the old log road. He tried to leap up but groaned and grabbed his right ankle. "Go on!" he urged, wincing with new pain.

"No! Here, let me help you up!"

★ ★

"No! No! You go on; get there and have them wait for me. I'll be right behind you."

Sarah looked doubtful, but Nat waved her on.

As she turned away, Nat said, "Give me that sheet. I can tie it around my ankle and hope that helps."

In a few seconds she was lost to sight in the mists and brush that lined the road. Nat started to fashion a support bandage on his ankle when he heard Sarah scream and a man's harsh voice.

"Hold still, you black runaway!" A loud slapping sound was followed by a moan from Sarah.

Cobb caught her! The terrible realization made Nat struggle to his feet, his face contorted with pain. He sank back onto the slippery, wet log, sick at heart.

"Now, girl," Cobb's voice came from beyond the brush growing across the road, "where's the boy?"

Nat couldn't hear if she answered, but he caught the heavy clumping of the slave hunter's boots on the log road. *He's coming!* Nat scooted off the road and into the heavy brush beside it, hindered by the sheet, which snagged on long thorns.

With racing heart Nat ripped the wet sheet free and started to drop it so he could scoot deeper into the brush. But he knew he could not really hide, that he would also be caught and miss escaping to freedom.

Wait! He stopped his fearful thoughts as he recalled something Sarah had said.

With frantic haste he fought to get the sheet spread out enough to struggle under it. He had just finished when he heard Cobb drag Sarah through the brush over the road. If Nat had not moved, he would have been in full sight of the slave catcher.

"Where'd he go?" Cobb said, more to himself than to Sarah.

Peeking through a tear in the sheet, Nat slowly stood up on his good leg. He opened his mouth and made the scariest voice possible. "Ohoooooo!"

★ ★

Cobb stopped abruptly, staring at the white apparition in the moonlight. "No!" he croaked, his voice breaking with fright. He released Sarah so suddenly, she fell to the log road. Cobb leaped back and dropped his gun. "Get away from me!"

Nat howled again, hoping to scare Cobb away for good. "Ohoooo!"

Sarah did not move as Cobb made a strangled sound and backed off the road. His eyes, wide in the moonlight, were locked on the wraith that suddenly seemed to have risen from the earth.

Cobb cried in a horrified voice at the ghostly form. "Don't come near me!"

"Ohoooo!"

"Leave me alone! Leave me alone!" Cobb whirled and plunged into the marsh. A frightened screech ripped through the swamp air, followed by the sound of Cobb frantically crashing through the underbrush.

Nat tore the wet sheet from over his head and dropped it on the road, where Sarah still lay. Reaching down, he helped her up. "Let me lean on you," he said, "and let's get out of here!"

"What happened?" Sarah asked, supporting Nat so he could hobble along the corduroy road.

"I believe," Nat replied with grim satisfaction, "that our superstitious Barley Cobb thinks he just met up with the ghost of Black Water Swamp!"

A few minutes later, the muddy, wet, and tired pair staggered out of the swamp toward the wagon waiting to take them on the first part of their trip to freedom.

★ ★ ★ ★ ★

Shortly after Nat and Sarah were safely hidden in the wagon's secret compartments, Emily watched the first probing shafts of sunlight make their silent way across the land. Her

★ ★

heart still raced over the close call the fugitives had had with Cobb and his hounds.

She tried to resist glancing back to see if anyone was following, but that was difficult. She wondered what would happen to her if they were stopped and the runaway slaves were found. She fretted that Nat's ankle could not be treated until dark when it would be safer.

Finally giving in to her urge, she looked back. There was no sign of anyone, although she could see a small grove of trees the team had recently passed. A heavy sigh escaped her as she again faced forward. There was now no hope of seeing Gideon. Maybe she would never again see him.

She shoved the depressing thought aside and absently removed her wide-brimmed hat to touch the pink ribbon that tied her hair back. Julie had been right; her neck was cooler this way.

Emily knew it was a long way to Richmond, and lots of things could happen before then. Still, she tried to relax, feeling more secure.

Five minutes passed in silence before a shout suddenly came from behind. Emily jumped in alarm and started to look back, but Mr. Yates dropped his near hand from the reins and grabbed her hand in warning.

"Don't look! Act as if we don't hear anything!"

A second shout made Emily cringe. "I hear hoofbeats. Someone's riding hard after us, but I only hear one horse!"

"It could be a patroller," Mr. Yates replied calmly. "We can't outrun him. If he stops us, try to be composed and natural. Let me do the talking."

"How about them?" Emily motioned with her chin toward the hidden compartment under their seat.

"They won't make a sound because they know what will happen to them if they're found."

"Hey, stop!" The cry from behind rose above the steady drumming of hoofbeats. "Emily, stop!"

★ ★

"Gideon?" She whirled around in surprise. "Mr. Yates, please stop! It's my friend Gideon!"

"We can't risk that. Wait until he gets close and then ask him to ride alongside while we keep moving."

She waved her hat in a broad, sweeping motion to acknowledge that Gideon had been seen, although the team didn't even slow up.

Mr. Yates cautioned, "Don't say anything about our packages."

Emily twisted around to the left as Gideon rode the mule alongside the wagon. She smiled at him.

Mr. Yates spoke before she could. "I can't stop. I've got to get these young trees out of the hot sun as soon as possible."

"It's all right, Mr. Yates." Gideon slowed his mount to match the team's pace. "Hello, Emily." He returned her smile. "I thought I had missed you."

"This is my only chance to get back to Illinois." She looked closely at him. "Are you all right?"

When Gideon didn't answer, Emily cried in dismay, "Something *is* wrong! You look as if you haven't slept for a week."

"Didn't sleep much last night." His tone was solemn, with all trace of a joyful smile gone.

"Your brother!" She reached out impulsively and touched Gideon's arm. "Did you find him? Is he well?"

"He was wounded, but he's going to recover." He choked off whatever else he wanted to say. "We both got home last night, but he has to go back to Camp Pickens in a few days."

"Then there's something else. What is it?"

"My father . . ." His voice broke as Emily sucked in her breath. Gideon rushed on, "He died last night."

"Oh no! I'm so sorry!"

"It happened shortly after Isham and I got home. It was very sudden; his heart." Tears formed in Gideon's eyes, and he dropped his head, filling her in on the details.

Emily said, "I wish I could stay and help, but I'm no longer

★ ★

welcome at Briarstone." She quickly told why, concluding, "Yet I would like to be with you and your family at this time."

"You're a good friend, Emily." His voice had a slight tremble. "But you have to go on to what's ahead for you, just as I have to do here."

He paused, then asked, "Are you ever coming back?"

"I doubt it," she said honestly. "Julie is the only one who wants me here."

Shyly, Gideon replied, "That's not quite true. Julie's not the only one."

Emily was deeply touched. "Thank you, Gideon."

"I'm not much of a hand at letters," he said, his tone brightening. "But I'll write if you will answer."

"Oh, I will. Though mail service has stopped between the Union and Confederacy, I've heard about private individuals with passes between North and South who will carry messages for a price. So write me in care of Jessie Barlow. I'll give you the address."

Gideon wanted to tell Emily what Brice Barlow had done for Isham, but now didn't seem to be the time. Instead, he said, "I don't have a pencil."

Emily turned to Mr. Yates. "Do you have one?"

"No, but when we get to Richmond, our friend where you're staying will have one. Give her your Illinois address, and I'll bring it back to Gideon."

"Good idea!" Emily agreed. "In case I have trouble getting a pass into Union lines, I would appreciate if you would give Gideon that woman's address, too."

"Thanks. There are a lot of things to tell you when I write." Gideon shifted in the saddle. "Now I've got to get home."

"I understand. I'm glad you caught up with us."

Gideon timidly suggested, "When the war is over, maybe we'll meet again."

"I hope so. Until then, I'll pray for you."

"And I'll do the same for you."

★ ★

Emily impulsively reached around and freed the pink ribbon from her hair. "Here," she said, handing it to him, "when you look at it, think that we will meet again. Let this also remind you to never give up on your dream about being a writer."

Gideon dropped his eyes, feeling that he could not tell her that his father's dying had also been the death of his writing dream. There was no one to run the farm except him. Then he remembered what Isham had said about going where bugles call. Gideon also heard that call. He would answer it later, but now he had other responsibilities.

He looked at Emily, his eyes again filling with hope. "Thanks," he said, lightly touching the ribbon. "I will remember, and someday I will be a writer." He turned Hercules around. "Someday, Emily, but good-bye for now." He rode fast toward home.

The wagon continued toward Richmond, but Emily kept looking back. Her vision blurred with unshed tears until Gideon started around a curve in the road. There he twisted in the saddle to look back at her.

Even through her tears, she saw him wave with her pink ribbon in his hand.

EPILOGUE

October 12, 1933

A mixture of sorrow and pride sweeps over me as I gently replace that once-pink ribbon in my boyhood journal. Another chapter was over, but it wasn't the end of the story. The war would last almost four more years.

There had been no great land battles in Virginia during the time of this adventure. However, that was about to change as the conflicts accelerated, and some hard new lessons were to be learned by individuals and a divided nation.

Emily, Nat, and I had been prepared for what happened next because of what each of us had already gone through.

Nat told me later that the teachings of his mother had proved that real strength is in the mind. That includes determination to never quit. It saved his life and Sarah's.

I learned that responsibility is a mark of growing up, which meant putting duty above personal desire. But my writing dream did not die, because long-term vision sees beyond today's troubles.

Emily said she had learned that integrity is doing what's right, no matter what the price. That was easier for her when she found strength through faith in the scriptural injunction, "Do what is right and good in the Lord's sight. . . ."

It has been truthfully said that life is about the only place where you get the test and then the lesson.

That was true when Emily, Nat, and I faced the next great adventures of growing up during the most savage war this country has ever known.

Emily was trapped in Richmond, the Confederate capital, when Union forces fought their way to within six miles of there.

Nat thought he was about to reach freedom until the Seven Days Campaign outside Richmond caught up with him.

As for me . . . well, Papa's death again triggered a challenge by William Lodge trying to get control of our family farm. Barley Cobb also posed a new, unexpected problem in the second year of the war.

I'll tell you about all of those events when again I open the pages of my boyhood journal to review *A Burden of Honor*.

Early Teen Fiction Series From
Bethany House Publishers
(Ages 11–14)

———— ∞ ————

BETWEEN TWO FLAGS • by Lee Roddy
Join Gideon, Emily, and Nat as they face the struggles
of growing up during the Civil War.

THE ALLISON CHRONICLES • by Melody Carlson
Follow along as Allison O'Brian, the daughter of a
famous 1940s movie star, searches for the truth about
her past and the love of a family.

HIGH HURDLES • by Lauraine Snelling
Show jumper DJ Randall strives to defy the odds and
achieve her dream of winning Olympic Gold.

SUMMERHILL SECRETS • by Beverly Lewis
Fun-loving Merry Hanson encounters mystery and
excitement in Pennsylvania's Amish country.

THE TIME NAVIGATORS • by Gilbert Morris
Travel back in time with Danny and Dixie as they
explore unforgettable moments in history.